A NEW RACE OF MEN

Chatvieux nodded. "The rest of us can put our heads together on leaving a record for these people. We'll micro-engrave the record on a set of corrosion-proof metal leaves, of a size our colonists can handle. We can tell them, very simply, what happened, and plant a few suggestions that there's more to the universe than what they find in the puddles."

"Question," Eunice Wagner said. "Are we going to tell them they're microscopic?"

"Yes, we are," Chatvieux said. "These people will be of the race of men, Eunice. We want them to wind their way back into the community of men . . . somehow."

Other SIGNET Science Fiction You'll Enjoy

The Seedling Stars

by James Blish

A SIGNET BOOK from
NEW AMERICAN LIBRARY
TIMES MIRROR

TO H. L. GOLD

© COPYRIGHT, 1957 BY JAMES BLISH

Book I of this volume was first published in
Fantasy and Science Fiction magazine as "A Time to Survive,"
and is copyright 1955 by Fantasy House, Inc.
Book II was first published in *IF Worlds of Science Fiction*
magazine and is copyright 1954 by Quinn Publishing Co., Inc.
Book III, in considerably different form, appeared in
Super Science Stories as "Sunken Universe," copyright 1942 by
Fictioneers, Inc., and in part in *Galaxy Science Fiction* as
"Surface Tension," copyright 1952 by the
Galaxy Publishing Corporation.
Book IV was first published in *IF Worlds of Science Fiction*
as "Watershed" and is copyright 1955 by
Quinn Publishing Co., Inc.

Published by arrangement with Gnome Press, Inc.

FOURTH PRINTING

SIGNET TRADEMARK REG. U.S. PAT. OFF. AND FOREIGN COUNTRIES
REGISTERED TRADEMARK——MARCA REGISTRADA
HECHO EN CHICAGO, U.S.A.

SIGNET, SIGNET CLASSICS, SIGNETTE, MENTOR AND PLUME BOOKS
*are published by The New American Library, Inc.,
1301 Avenue of the Americas, New York, New York 10019*

FIRST PRINTING, FEBRUARY, 1959

PRINTED IN THE UNITED STATES OF AMERICA

The
Seedling
Stars

BOOK ONE

SEEDING PROGRAM

1

The spaceship resumed humming around Sweeney without his noticing the change. When Capt. Meiklejon's voice finally came again from the wall speaker, Sweeney was still lying buckled to his bunk in a curious state of tranquillity he had never known before, and couldn't possibly have described, even to himself. Though he had a pulse, he might otherwise have concluded that he was dead. It took him several minutes to respond.

"Sweeney, do you hear me? Are—you all right?"

The brief hesitation in the pilot's breathing made Sweeney grin. From Meiklejon's point of view, and that of most of the rest of humanity, Sweeney was all wrong. He was, in fact, dead.

The heavily insulated cabin, with its own airlock to the outside, and no access for Sweeney at all to the rest of the ship, was a testimonial to his wrongness. So was Meiklejon's tone: the voice of a man addressing, not another human being, but something that had to be kept in a vault.

A vault designed to protect the universe outside it—not to protect its contents from the universe.

"Sure, I'm all right," Sweeney said, snapping the buckle and sitting up. He checked the thermometer, which still registered its undeviating minus 194° F.—the mean surface temperature of Ganymede, moon number III of Jupiter. "I was dozing, sort of. What's up?"

"I'm putting the ship into her orbit; we're about a thousand miles up from the satellite now. I thought you might want to take a look."

"Sure enough. Thanks, Mickey."

The wall speaker said, "Yeah. Talk to you later." Sweeney grappled for the guide rail and pulled himself over to the cabin's single bull'seye port, maneuvering with considerable precision. For a man to whom 1/6 Earth gravity is normal, free fall—a situation of no gravity at all—is only an extreme case.

Which was what Sweeney was, too. A human being—but an extreme case.

He looked out. He knew exactly what he would see; he had studied it exhaustively from photos, from teletapes, from maps, and through telescopes both at home on the Moon and on Mars. When you approach Ganymede at inferior conjunction, as Meiklejon was doing, the first thing that hits you in the eye is the huge oval blot called Neptune's Trident—so named by the earliest Jovian explorers because it was marked with the Greek letter *psi* on the old Howe composite map. The name had turned out to have been well chosen: that blot is a deep, many-pronged sea, largest at the eastern end, which runs from about 120° to 165° in longitude, and from about 10° to 33° North latitude. A sea of what? Oh, water, of course—water frozen rock-solid forever, and covered with a layer of rock-dust about three inches thick.

East of the Trident, and running all the way north to the pole, is a great triangular marking called the Gouge, a torn-up, root-entwined, avalanche-shaken valley which continues right around the pole and back up into the other hemisphere, fanning out as it goes. (*Up* because north to space pilots, as to astronomers, is down.) There is nothing quite like the Gouge on any other planet, although at inferior conjunction, when your ship is coming down on Ganymede at the 180° meridian, it is likely to remind you of Syrtis Major on Mars.

There is, however, no real resemblance. Syrtis Major is perhaps the pleasantest land on all of Mars. The Gouge, on the other hand, is—a gouge.

On the eastern rim of this enormous scar, at long. 218°, N. lat. 32°, is an isolated mountain about 9,000 feet high, which had no name as far as Sweeney knew; it was marked with the letter *pi* on the Howe map. Because of its isolation, it can be seen easily from Earth's Moon in a good telescope when the sunrise terminator lies in that longitude, its peak shining detached in the darkness like a little star. A semicircular shelf juts westward out over the Gouge from the base of Howe's *pi*, it sides bafflingly sheer for a world which shows no other signs of folded strata.

It was on that shelf that the other Adapted Men lived.

Sweeney stared down at the nearly invisible mountain with its star-fire peak for a long time, wondering why he was not reacting. Any appropriate emotion would do: anticipation, alarm, eagerness, anything at all, even fear. For that matter, having been locked up in a safe for over two months should by now have driven him foaming to get out, even if only to join the Adapted Men. Instead, the tranquillity persisted. He was unable to summon more than a momentary curiosity over Howe's *pi* before his eye was drawn away to Jupiter himself, looming monstrous and insanely-colored only 600,000 miles away, give or take a few thousand. And even that planet had attracted him only because it was brighter; otherwise, it had no meaning.

"Mickey?" he said, forcing himself to look back down into the Gouge.

"Right here, Sweeney. How does it look?"

"Oh, like a relief map. That's how they all look. Where are you going to put me down? Don't the orders leave it up to us?"

"Yeah. But I don't think there's any choice," Meiklejon's voice said, less hesitantly. "It'll have to be the big plateau— Howe's H."

Sweeney scanned the oval mare with a mild distaste. Standing on that, he would be as conspicuous as if he'd been planted in the middle of the Moon's Mare Crisium. He said so.

"You've no choice," Meiklejon repeated calmly. He burped the rockets several times. Sweeney's weight returned briefly, tried to decide which way it wanted to throw itself, and then went away again. The ship was now in its orbit; but whether Meiklejon had set it up to remain put over its present co-ordinates, or instead it was to cruise criss-cross over the whole face of the satellite, Sweeney couldn't tell, and didn't ask. The less he knew about that, the better.

"Well, it's a long drop," Sweeney said. "And that atmosphere isn't exactly the thickest in the system. I'll have to fall in the lee of the mountain. I don't want to have to trudge a couple of hundred miles over Howe's H."

"On the other hand," Meiklejon said, "if you come down too close, our friends down there will spot your parachute. Maybe it'd be better if we dropped you into the Gouge, after all. There's so much tumbled junk down there that the radar echoes must be tremendous—not a chance of their spotting a little thing like a man on a parachute."

"*No*, thank you. There's still optical spotting, and a foil parachute looks nothing like a rock spur, even to an Adapted Man. It'll have to be behind the mountain, where I'm in both optical *and* radar shadow at once. Besides, how could I climb out of the Gouge onto the shelf? They didn't plant themselves on the edge of a cliff for nothing."

"That's right," Meiklejon said. "Well, I've got the catapult pointed. I'll suit up and join you on the hull."

"All right. Tell me again just what you're going to do while I'm gone, so I won't find myself blowing the whistle when you're nowhere around." The sound of a suit locker being opened came tinnily over the intercom. Sweeney's chute harness was already strapped on, and getting the respirator and throat-mikes into place would only take a moment. Sweeney needed no other protection.

"I'm to stay up here with all power off except maintenance for 300 days," Meiklejon's voice, sounding more distant now, was repeating. "Supposedly by that time you'll have worked yourself in good with our friends down there and will know the setup. I stand ready to get a message from you on a fixed frequency. You're to send me only a set of code letters; I feed them into the computer, the comp tells me what to do and I act accordingly. If I don't hear from you after 300 days, I utter a brief but heartfelt prayer and go home. Beyond that, God help me, I don't know a thing."

"That's plenty," Sweeney told him. "Let's go."

Sweeney went out his personal airlock. Like all true interplanetary craft, Meiklejon's ship had no overall hull. She consisted of her essential components, including the personnel globe, held together by a visible framework of girders and I-beams. It was one of the longest of the latter, one which was already pointed toward Howe's H, which would serve as the "catapult."

Sweeney looked up at the globe of the satellite. The old familiar feeling of falling came over him for a moment; he looked down, reorienting himself to the ship, until it went away. He'd be going in that direction soon enough.

Meiklejon came around the bulge of the personnel globe, sliding his shoes along the metal. In his bulky, misshapen spacesuit, it was he who looked like the unhuman member of the duo.

"Ready?" he said.

Sweeney nodded and lay face down on the I-beam, snapping the guide-clips on his harness into place around it. He could feel Meiklejon's mitts at his back, fastening the JATO unit; he could see nothing now, however, but the wooden sled that would protect his body from the beam.

"Okay," the pilot said. "Good luck, Sweeney."

"Thanks. Count me off, Mickey."

"Coming up on five seconds. Five. Four. Three. Two. One. *Hack.*"

The JATO unit shuddered and dealt Sweeney a nearly paralyzing blow between his shoulder-blades. For an instant the acceleration drove him down into his harness, and the sled spraddled against the metal of the I-beam.

Then, suddenly, the vibration stopped. He was flying free. A little belatedly, he jerked the release ring.

The sled went curving away from under him, dwindling rapidly among the stars. The pressure at his back cut out as the JATO unit, still under power, flamed ahead of him. The instantly-dissipated flick of heat from its exhaust made him ill for a moment; then it had vanished. It would hit too hard to leave anything where it landed but a hole.

Nothing was left but Sweeney, falling toward Ganymede, head first.

From almost the beginning, from that day unrememberably early in his childhood when he had first realized that the underground dome on the Moon was all there was to the universe for nobody but himself, Sweeney had wanted to be human; wanted it with a vague, impersonal ache which set quickly into a chill bitterness of manner and outlook at his unique everyday life, and in dreams with flares of searing loneliness which became more infrequent but also more intense as he matured, until such a night would leave him as shaken and mute, sometimes for several days at a stretch, as an escape from a major accident.

The cadre of psychologists, psychiatrists and analysts assigned to him did what they could, but that was not very much. Sweeney's history contained almost nothing that was manipulable by any system of psychotherapy developed to help human beings. Nor were the members of the cadre ever able to agree among themselves what the prime goal of such therapy should be: whether to help Sweeney to live with the facts of his essential inhumanity, or to fan instead that single spark of hope which the non-medical people on the Moon were constantly holding out toward Sweeney as the sole reason for his existence.

The facts were simple and implacable. Sweeney was an Adapted Man—adapted, in this instance, to the bitter cold, the light gravity, and the thin stink of atmosphere which prevailed on Ganymede. The blood that ran in his veins, and the sol substrate of his every cell, was nine-tenths liquid ammonia; his bones were Ice IV; his respiration was a complex hydrogen-to-methane cycle based not upon catalysis by an iron-bearing pigment, but upon the locking and unlocking of a double sulfur bond; and he could survive for weeks, if he had to, upon a diet of rock dust.

He had always been this way. What had made him so had happened to him literally before he had been conceived: the application, to the germ cells which had later united to form him, of an elaborate constellation of techniques—selective mitotic poisoning, pinpoint X-irradiation, tectogenetic microsurgery, competitive metabolic inhibition, and perhaps fifty more whose names he had never even heard—which collectively had been christened "pantropy." The word, freely retranslated, meant "changing everything"—and it fitted.

As the pantropists had changed in advance the human pattern in Sweeney's shape and chemistry, so they had changed his education, his world, his thoughts, even his ancestors. You didn't make an Adapted Man with just a wave of the wand, Dr. Alfven had once explained proudly to Sweeney over the intercom. Even the ultimate germ cells were the emergents of a hundred previous generations, bred one from another before they had passed the zygote stage like one-celled animals, each one biassed a little farther toward the cyanide and ice and everything nice that little boys like Sweeney were made of. The psych cadre picked off Dr. Alfven at the end of that same week, at the regular review of the tapes of what had been said to Sweeney and what he had found to say back, but they need hardly have taken the trouble. Sweeney had never heard a nursery rhyme, any more than he had ever experienced the birth trauma or been exposed to the Oedipus complex. He was a law unto himself, with most of the whereases blank.

He noticed, of course, that Alfven failed to show up when his next round was due, but this was commonplace. Scientists came and went around the great sealed cavern, always accompanied by the polite and beautifully uniformed private police of the Greater Earth Port Authority, but they rarely lasted very long. Even among the psych cadre there was always a peculiar tension, a furious constraint which erupted periodically into pitched shouting battles. Sweeney never found out what the shouting was about because the sound to the outside was always cut as soon as the quarrels began, but he noticed that some of the participants never showed up again.

"Where's Dr. Emory? Isn't this his day?"

"He finished his tour of duty."

"But I want to talk to him. He promised to bring me a book. Won't he be back for a visit?"

"I don't think so, Sweeney. He's retired. Don't worry about him, he'll get along just fine. I'll bring you your book."

It was after the third of these incidents that Sweeney was let out on the surface of the Moon for the first time — guarded, it was true, by five men in spacesuits, but Sweeney didn't care. The new freedom seemed enormous to him, and his own suit, only a token compared to what the Port cops had to wear, hardly seemed to exist. It was his first foretaste of the liberty he was to have, if the many hints could be trusted, after his job was done. He could even see the Earth, where people lived.

About the job he knew everything there was to know, and knew it as second nature. It had been drummed into him from his cold and lonely infancy, always with the same command at the end:

"We must have those men back."

Those six words were the reason for Sweeney; they were also Sweeney's sole hope. The Adapted Men had to be recaptured and brought back to Earth—or more exactly, back to the dome on the Moon, the only place besides Ganymede where they could be kept alive. And if they could not all be recaptured—he was to entertain this only as a possibility—he must at least come back with Dr. Jacob Rullman. Only Rullman would be sure to know the ultimate secret: how to turn an Adapted Man back into a human being.

Sweeney understood that Rullman and his associates were criminals, but how grievous their crime had been was a question he had never tried to answer for himself. His standards were too sketchy. It was clear from the beginning, however, that the colony on Ganymede had been set up without Earth's sanction, by methods of which Earth did not approve (except for special cases like Sweeney), and that Earth wanted it broken up. Not by force, for Earth wanted to know first what Rullman knew, but by the elaborate artifice which was Sweeney himself.

We must have those men back. After that, the hints said— never promising anything directly—Sweeney could be made human, and know a better freedom than walking the airless surface of the Moon with five guards.

It was usually after one of these hints that one of those suddenly soundless quarrels would break out among the staff. Any man of normal intelligence would have come to suspect that the hints were less than well founded upon any real expectation, and Sweeney's training helped to make him suspicious early; but in the long run he did not care. The hints offered his only hope and he accepted them with hope but without expectation. Besides, the few opening words of such quarrels which he had overheard before the intercom clicked off had suggested that there was more to the disagreement than simple doubt of the convertibility of an Adapted Man. It had been Emory, for instance, who had burst out unexpectedly and explosively:

"But suppose Rullman was right—?"

Click.

Right about what? Is a lawbreaker ever "right?" Sweeney could not know. Then there had been the technie who had said "It's the cost that's the trouble with terra-forming"— what did that mean?—and had been hustled out of the monitoring chamber on some trumped-up errand hardly a minute later. There were many such instances, but inevitably Sweeney failed to put the fragments together into any pattern. He decided only that they did not bear directly upon his chances of becoming human, and promptly abandoned them in the vast desert of his general ignorance.

In the long run, only the command was real—the command and the nightmares. *We must have those men back.* Those six words were the reason why Sweeney, like a man whose last effort to awaken has failed, was falling head first toward Ganymede.

The Adapted Men found Sweeney halfway up the great col which provided the only access to their cliff-edge colony from the plateau of Howe's H. He did not recognize them; they conformed to none of the photographs he had memorized; but they accepted his story readily enough. And he had not needed to pretend exhaustion—Ganymede's gravity was normal to him, but it had been a long trek and a longer climb.

He was surprised to find, nevertheless, that he had enjoyed it. For the first time in his life he had walked unguarded, either by men or by mechanisms, on a world where he felt physically at home; a world without walls, a world where he was essentially alone. The air was rich and pleasant, the winds came from wherever they chose to blow, the temperature in the col was considerably below what had been allowable in the dome on the Moon, and there was sky all around him, tinged with indigo and speckled with stars that twinkled now and then.

He would have to be careful. It would be all too easy to

accept Ganymede as home. He had been warned against that, but somehow he had failed to realize that the danger would be not merely real, but—seductive.

The young men took him swiftly the rest of the way to the colony. They had been as incurious as they had been anonymous. Rullman was different. The look of stunned disbelief on the scientist's face, as Sweeney was led into his high-ceilinged, rock-walled office, was so total as to be frightening. He said: "What's this!"

"We found him climbing the col. We thought he'd gotten lost, but he says he belongs to the parent flight."

"Impossible," Rullman said. "Quite impossible." And then he fell silent, studying the newcomer from crown to toe. The expression of shock dimmed only slightly.

The long scrutiny gave Sweeney time to look back. Rullman was older than his pictures, but that was natural; if anything, he looked a little less marked by age than Sweeney had anticipated. He was spare, partly bald, and slope-shouldered, but the comfortable pod under his belt-line which had shown in the photos was almost gone now. Evidently living on Ganymede had hardened him some. The pictures had failed to prepare Sweeney for the man's eyes: they were as hooded and unsettling as an owl's.

"You'd better tell me who you are," Rullman said at last. "And how you got here. You aren't one of us, that's certain."

"I'm Donald Leverault Sweeney," Sweeney said. "Maybe I'm not one of you, but my mother said I was. I got here in her ship. She said you'd take me in."

Rullman shook his head. "That's impossible, too. Excuse me, Mr. Sweeney, but you've probably no idea what a bombshell you are. You must be Shirley Leverault's child, then—but how did you get here? How did you survive all this time? Who kept you alive, and tended you, after we left the Moon? And above all, how did you get away from the Port cops? We knew that Port Earth found our Moon lab even before we abandoned it. I can hardly believe that you even exist."

Nevertheless, the scientist's expression of flat incredulity was softening moment by moment. He was, Sweeney judged, already beginning to buy it. And necessarily: there Sweeney stood before him, breathing Ganymede's air, standing easily in Ganymede's gravity, with Ganymede's dust on his cold skin, a fact among inarguable facts.

"The Port cops found the big dome, all right," Sweeney said. "But they never found the little one, the pilot plant. Dad blew up the tunnel between the two before they landed—he

15

was killed in the rock-slide. Of course I was still just a cell in a jug when that happened."

"I see," Rullman said thoughtfully. "We picked up an explosion on our ship's instruments before we took off. But we thought it was the Port raiders beginning to bomb, unexpected though that was. Then they didn't destroy the big lab either, after all?"

"No," Sweeney said. Rullman surely must know that; radio talk between Earth and Moon must be detectable at least occasionally out here. "There were still some intercom lines left through to there; my mother used to spend a lot of time listening in on what was going on. So did I, after I was old enough to understand it. That was how we found out that the Ganymedian colony hadn't been bombed out, either."

"But where did you get your power?"

"Most of it from our own strontium^{90} cell. Everything was shielded so the cops couldn't detect any stray fields. When the cell finally began to give out, we had to tap Port's main accumulator line—just for a little bit at first, but the drain kept going up." He shrugged. "Sooner or later they were bound to spot it—and did."

Rullman was momentarily silent, and Sweeney knew that he was doing the pertinent arithmetic in his head, comparing the 20-year half-life of strontium^{90} with Sweeney's and the Adapted Men's chronology. The figures would jibe, of course. The Port cops' briefing had been thorough about little details like that.

"It's still quite astounding, having to rethink this whole episode after so many years," Rullman said. "With all due respect, Mr. Sweeney, it's hard to imagine Shirley Leverault going through such an ordeal—and all alone, too, except for a child she could never even touch, a child as difficult and technical to tend as an atomic pile. I remember her as a frail, low-spirited girl, trailing along after us listlessly because Robert was in the project." He frowned reminiscently. "She used to say, 'It's his job.' She never thought of it as anything more than that."

"*I* was her job," Sweeney said evenly. The Port cops had tried to train him to speak bitterly when he mentioned his mother, but he had never been able to capture the emotion that they wanted him to imitate. He had found, however, that if he rapped out the syllables almost without inflection, they were satisfied with the effect. "You misjudged her, Dr. Rullman—or else she changed after Dad was killed. She had guts enough for ten. And she got paid for it in the end. In the only coin the Port cops know how to pay."

"I'm sorry," Rullman said gently. "But at least you got away. I'm sure that's as she would have wanted it. Where did the ship you spoke of come from?"

"Why, we always had it. It belonged to Dad, I suppose. It was stored in a natural chimney near our dome. When the cops broke into the monitoring room, I went out the other side of the dome, while they were—busy with mother, and beat it. There wasn't anything I could have done—"

"Of course, of course," Rullman said, his voice low and quiet. "You wouldn't have lasted a second in their air. You did the right thing. Go on."

"Well, I got to the ship and got it off. I didn't have time to save anything but myself. They followed me all the way, but they didn't shoot. I think there's still one of them upstairs now."

"We'll sweep for him, but there's nothing we can do about him in any case except keep him located. You bailed out, I gather."

"Yes. Otherwise I wouldn't have had a chance—they seemed to want me back in the worst way. They must have the ship by now, and the coordinates for the colony too."

"Oh, they've had those coordinates since we first landed," Rullman said. "You were lucky, Mr. Sweeney, and bold, too. You bring back a sense of immediacy that I haven't felt for years, since our first escape. But there's one more problem."

"What is it? If I can help—"

"There's a test we'll have to make," Rullman said. "Your story seems to hold water; and I really don't see how you could have become what you are, unless you were really one of us. But we have to be certain."

"Sure," Sweeney said. "Let's go."

Rullman beckoned and led him out of the office through a low stone door. The corridor through which they passed was so like all those Sweeney had seen on the Moon that he scarcely bothered to notice it. Even the natural gravity and circulating, unprocessed air were soothing rather than distracting. It was the test that worried Sweeney, precisely because he knew that he would be helpless to affect the outcome. Either the Port Authority's experts had put him together cunningly enough to pass any test, or—

—or he would never have the chance to become human.

Rullman nodded Sweeney through another door into a long, low-ceilinged room furnished with half a dozen laboratory benches and a good deal of glassware. The air was more active here; as on the Moon, there were ventilators roiling it. Someone came around a towering, twisted fractionating apparatus in which many small bubbles orbited, and moved toward them. It was, Sweeney saw, a small glossy-haired girl, with white hands and dark eyes and delicately precise feet. She was wearing the typical technie's white jacket, and a plum-colored skirt.

"Hello, Dr. Rullman. Can I help?"

"Sure, if you can neglect that percolator a while, Mike. I want to run an ID typing; we've got a new man here. All right?"

"Oh, I think so. It'll take a minute to get the sera out." She moved away from them to another desk and began to take out ampoules and shake them before a hooded light. Sweeney watched her. He had seen female technies before, but none so modelled, so unconstrained, or so—close as this. He felt light-headed, and hoped that he would not be asked to speak for a little while. There was sweat on his palms and a mumbling of blood in his inner ear, and he thought perhaps he might cry.

He had been plunged into the midst of his untested, long-delayed adolescence, and he liked it no better than anyone ever had.

But his diamond-etched caution did not blur completely. He remembered to remember that the girl had been as little surprised to see him as the two young men who had found him climbing the col had been. Why? Surely Dr. Rullman was not the only Adapted Man to know everyone in the colony by sight, and hence the only one able to feel consternation at the sight of a strange face. By this time, the settlers on Ganymede should know each other's slightest wrinkles, should have committed to memory every gesture, mannerism, dimple, shading, flaw or virtue that would help them to tell each other from the hostile remainder of overwhelming mankind.

The girl took Sweeney's hand, and for a moment the train of thought fell apart completely. Then there was a sharp stab in the tip of his right middle finger, and Mike was expressing droplets of blood into little puddles of bluish solution, spotted in sets of three on a great many slips of thin glass. Microscope slides; Sweeney had seen them before. As for the blood, she could have more if she wanted it.

But he returned doggedly to the question. Why had the young men and Mike failed to be surprised by Sweeney? Was it their age-group that counted? The original colonists of Ganymede would know both each other and their children by sight, while the youngsters to whom everything was essentially new would see nothing strange in a new face.

Children: then the colonists were fertile. There had never

18

been a hint of that, back on the Moon. Of course it meant nothing to Sweeney personally. Not a thing.

"Why, you're trembling," the girl said in a troubled voice. "It was only a little nick. You'd better sit down."

"Of course," Rullman said immediately. "You've been under quite a strain, Mr. Sweeney; forgive me for being so thoughtless. This will be over in just a moment."

Sweeney sat down gratefully and tried to think about nothing. Both the girl and Rullman were now also seated, at the bench, examining with microscopes the little puddles of diluted blood Mike had taken from Sweeney.

"Type O, Rh negative," the girl said. Rullman was taking notes. "MsMs, P negative, cdE/cde, Lutheran a-negative, Kell-Cellano negative, Lewis a-minus b-plus."

"Hmm," Rullman said, unilluminatingly, all as one sound. "Also Duffy a-negative, Jk-a, U positive, Jay positive, Bradbury-immune, platelets IV, and non-sickling. A pretty clean sweep. Mean anything to you, Mike?"

"It should," she said, looking at Sweeney speculatively. "You want me to match him, then."

Rullman nodded. The girl came to Sweeney's side and the spring-driven lancet went *snick* against another of his fingertips. After she went back to the bench, Sweeney heard the sound again, and saw her brush her own left middle fingertip against a slide. Silence.

"Compatible, Dr. Rullman."

Rullman turned to Sweeney and smiled for the first time. "You pass," he said. He seemed genuinely glad. "Welcome, Mr. Sweeney. Now if you'll come back to my office, we'll see what we can do about placing you in living quarters, and of course in a job—we've plenty of those. Thanks, Mike."

"You're welcome. Goodbye, Mr. Sweeney. It looks like I'll be seeing a lot more of you."

Sweeney nodded and gulped. It was not until he was back in Rullman's office that he could control his voice.

"What was that all about, Dr. Rullman? I mean, I know you were typing my blood, but what did it tell you?"

"It told me your *bona fides*," Rullman said. "Blood groups are inheritable; they follow the Mendelian laws very strictly. Your blood pattern gave me your identity, not as an individual, but as a member of a family. In other words, they showed that you really are what you claim to be, a descendant of Bob Sweeney and Shirley Leverault."

"I see. But you matched me against the girl, too. What did that test?"

"The so-called private factors, the ones that appear only

19

within a family and not in the general population," Rullman said. "You see, Mr. Sweeney, as we reckon such matters here, Michaela Leverault is your niece."

2

For at least the tenth time in two months, Mike was looking at Sweeney with astonishment, troubled and amused at once. "Now where," she said, "did you get *that* idea?"

The question, as usual, was dangerous, but Sweeney took his time. Mike knew that he was always slow to answer questions, and sometimes seemed not to hear them at all. The need for such a protective habit was luridly obvious to Sweeney, and he was only postponing the moment when it should become just as obvious to the Ganymedians; only the plainly pathological introversion of his character as a whole had excused him even thus far from a suspicion that he was ducking the hard ones.

Sooner or later, Sweeney was sure, that suspicion would arise. Sweeney had had no experience of women, but he was nevertheless convinced that Mike was an exceptional sample. Her quickness of penetration sometimes seemed close to telepathy. He mulled the question, leaning on the railing around the hedge below the mountain, looking reflectively into the Gouge, constructing his answer. Each day he had to shorten that mulling-time, though the questions grew no less difficult for his pains.

"From the Port cops," he said. "I've got only two answers to that question, Mike. Anything I didn't get from my mother, I got from spying on the cops."

Mike, too, looked down into the mists of the Gouge. It was a warm summer day, and a long one—three and a half Earth days long, while the satellite was on the sunward side of Jupiter, and coming, with Jupiter, closer and closer to the sun. The wind which blew over the flute-mouthpiece of rock on this side of the mountain was as gentle and variable as a flautist's breath, and did not stir the enormous tangled stolons and runners which filled the bottom of the great valley, or the wrap-around leaves which were plastered to them like so many thousands of blue-green Möbius strips.

It was not quiet down there, but it seemed quiet. There were many more thrums and rummums of rolling rocks and distant avalanches than one heard during the cold weather. The granite-skinned roots were growing rapidly while their short time was come, burrowing insistently into the walls of the valley, starting new trees and new rocks. In the cliffs, the warm weather changed water-of-crystallization from Ice IV to Ice III, the bound water snapping suddenly from one volume to another, breaking the rock strata apart. Sweeney knew how that worked; that was exfoliation; it was common on the Moon, though on the Moon it was caused by the re-freezing of Ice I in the gypsum strata. But the end-result was the same: rock-slides.

All these incessant erratic rumbles and muted thunders were the sounds of high summer in the Gouge. They were as peaceful to Sweeney's ears as bee-buzz is to an Earthman, though Sweeney had never encountered bee-buzz except in books. And like growing things everywhere, the terrific gnarled creepers down below sent up into the Adapted Men's air a fresh complacent odor, the specific smell of vegetable battle-unto-death which lulls animal nostrils and animal glands into forgetting past struggles of their own.

Ganymede was, as a matter of fact, a delightful world, even for a dead man. Or solely for a dead man.

"I can't understand why the Port cops would waste time batting lies back and forth," Mike said at last. "*They* know we weren't doing any commerce-raiding. We've never been so much as off Ganymede since we landed here. And we couldn't get off if we wanted to, now. Why should they pretend that we did? Why would they talk about it as if it was a fact, especially since they didn't know you were listening? It's senseless."

"I don't know," Sweeney said. "It never entered my head that you *weren't* commerce-raiding. If I'd had any notion that they weren't telling the truth, I'd have listened for clues to tell me why they weren't. But it never entered my head. And now it's too late; all I can do is guess."

"You must have heard something. Something you don't remember consciously. I can guess, too, but it's your guess that's important. You were listening to them; I wasn't. Try, Don."

"Well," Sweeney said, "maybe they didn't know that what they were saying was untrue. There's no law that says a Port cop has to be told the truth by his bosses. They're back on Earth; I was on the Moon, and so were they. And they sounded pretty convinced; the subject kept coming up, all the time, just casually, as if everybody knew about it. They all believed that Ganymede was raiding passenger liners as far in as the orbit of Mars. It was a settled fact. That's how I heard it."

"That fits," Mike said. Nevertheless, she was not looking at Sweeney; instead, she bent her head farther down over the rim of the Gouge, her hands locked together before her in dim space, until her small breasts were resting lightly on the railing. Sweeney took a long breath. The effluvium of the vines suddenly seemed anything but lulling.

"Tell me, Don," she said. "When did you hear the cops begin to talk this subject up? For the first time, I mean?"

His veering attention snapped back into the frigid center of his being so suddenly that it left behind a bright weal, as if a lash had been laid across his exposed brain. Mike was dangerous; dangerous. He had to remember that.

"When?" he said. "I don't know, Mike. The days were all alike. It was toward the end, I think. When I was a kid I used to hear them talk about us as if we were criminals, but I couldn't figure out why. I guessed that it was because we were different, that's all. It was only at the end that they began to talk about specific crimes, and even then it didn't make much sense to me. My mother and I hadn't ever pirated any ships, that was for sure."

"Only at the last. That's what I thought. They began to talk like that for the first time when your power began to fail. Isn't that right?"

Sweeney gave that one a long think, at least twice as long as would ordinarily have been safe before Mike. He already knew where Mike's questions were leading him. In this instance, a quick answer would be fatal. He had to appear to be attempting, with some pain, to dredge up information which was meaningless to him. After a while, he said:

"Yes, it was about then. I was beginning to cut down on tapping their calls; it didn't take much power, but we needed all we had. Maybe I missed hearing the important parts; that's possible."

"No," Mike said grimly. "I think you heard all of it. Or all you were meant to hear. And I think you interpreted what you heard in exactly the way they wanted you to, Don."

"It could be," Sweeney said slowly. "I was only a kid. I would have taken what I heard at face value. But that would mean that they knew we were there. I wonder. I don't remember exactly, but I don't think we had begun to sneak power from them yet. We were still thinking about putting a sun-cell on the surface, in those days."

"No, no. They must have known you were there years before you began to tap their power. Rullman's been talking about that lately. There are simple ways of detecting even a phone-line tap, and your strontium battery couldn't have been undetected very long, either. They waited only until they could be sure they'd get you when they finally raided you. It's the way they think. In the meantime, they fed you hokum when you eavesdropped."

So much for the story the cops had told Sweeney to tell. Only the extreme of stupidity which it assumed in the Adapted Men had protected it this long; nobody defends himself, at least at first, upon the assumption that his opponent thinks he is a microcephalic idiot. The deception had lasted two months, but it would never last 300 days.

"Why would they do that?" Sweeney said. "They were going to kill us as soon as they could—as soon as they could work out a way to do it without damaging our equipment. What did they care what we thought?"

"Torture," Mike said, straightening and locking her hands around the railing with the automatic tetany of a bird's claws touching a perch. She looked across the Gouge at the distant, heaped range on the other side. "They wanted you to think that everything your people had planned and done had come to nothing—that we had wound up as nothing but vicious criminals. Since they couldn't get to you and your mother immediately, they amused themselves with strafing you while they worked. Maybe they thought it'd help soften you up—goad you into making some mistake that would make the job of getting in to you easier. Or maybe they did it just because they enjoyed it. Because it made them feel good."

After a short silence, Sweeney said, "Maybe that was it. Maybe not. I don't know, Mike."

She turned to him suddenly and took him by the shoulders. Her eyes were crystal blue. "How could you know?" she said, her fingers digging into his deltoid muscles. "How could you know *anything* when there was nobody to tell you? The Earth must be full of lies about us now—lies, and nothing but lies! You've got to forget them—forget them all—just as though you'd just been born. You *have* just been born, Don, believe me. Only just. What they fed you on the Moon was lies; you've got to start learning the truth here, learning it from the beginning, like a child!"

She held him a moment longer. She was actually shaking him. Sweeney did not know what to say; he did not even know what emotion to mimic. The emotion he felt was still almost unknown; he did not dare let it show, let alone let it loose. While the girl looked furiously into his eyes, he could not even blink.

After all, he really had been born some time ago. Born dead.

The painful, tenfold pressure on his shoulders changed suddenly to a residual tingling over a deep ache, and Mike's hands dropped to her sides. She looked away, across the Gouge again. "It's no use," she said indistinctly. "I'm sorry. That's a hell of a way for a girl to talk to her uncle."

"That's all right, Mike. I was interested."

"I'm sure of it. . . . Let's go for a walk, Don. I'm sick of looking into the Gouge." She was already striding back toward the looming mountain under which the colony lived.

Sweeney watched her go, his icy blood sighing in his ears. It was terrible to be unable to think; he had never known the dizziness of it until he had met Mike Leverault, but now it seemed determined never to leave him—it abated sometimes, but it never quite went away. He had been ruefully glad, at the very beginning, that the close "blood" tie between himself and Mike, a genetic tie which was quite real since he was in fact Shirley Leverault's Adapted son, would prevent his becoming interested in the girl in accordance with Earth custom. But in fact it had had no such effect. Earth tabus had no force for him, and here on Ganymede, that particular tabu had been jettisoned summarily. Rullman had told him why.

"Don't give it a second thought," he had said on that very first day, grinning into Sweeney's stunned face. "We haven't any genetic reasons for forbidding inbreeding; quite the contrary. In a small group like ours, the strongest and most immediate evolutionary influence is genetic drift. Unless we took steps to prevent it, there'd be a loss of unfixed genes with every new generation. Obviously we can't allow that, or we'd wind up with a group in which there'd be no real individuals: everybody would be alike in some crucial and absolutely unpredictable respect. No tabu is worth that kind of outcome."

Rullman had gone on from there. He had said that simply permitting inbreeding could not in itself halt genetic drift; that in some respects it encouraged it; and that the colony was taking positive measures to circumvent drift, measures which would begin to bear fruit within eight generations. He had begun by this time to talk in terms of alleles and isomorphs and lethal recessives, and to scribble such cryptograms as $rrR{:}rRR/('rA)rr/R'Rr$ on the sheet of mica before him; and then, suddenly, he had looked up and realized that he had lost his audience. That, too, had amused him.

Sweeney had not minded. He knew he was ignorant. Besides, the colony's plans meant nothing to him; he was on

Ganymede to bring the colony to an end. As far as Mike was concerned, he knew that nothing would govern him but his monumental loneliness, as it governed everything else that he did and felt.

But he had been astonished to discover that, covertly at least, that same loneliness governed everyone else in the colony, with the sole possible exception of Rullman.

Mike looked back, and then, her face hardening, quickened her pace. Sweeney followed, as he knew he had to; but he was still struggling to think.

Much of what he had learned about the colony, if it was true—and at least everything he had been able to check had passed that test—had involved his unlearning what he had been taught by the Port cops. The cops, for instance, had said that the alleged commerce-raiding had had two purposes: secondarily to replenish food and equipment, but primarily to augment the colonists' numbers by capturing normal people for Adaptation.

There was no commerce-raiding going on now, that much was certain, and Sweeney was inclined to believe Mike's denial that there had ever been any in the past. Once one understood the ballistics of space-travel, one understood also that piracy is an impossible undertaking, simply because it is more work than it is worth. But beyond this persuasive practical objection, there was the impossibility of the motive the Port cops had imputed to the Ganymedians. The primary purpose was nonsense. The colonists were fertile, and hence did not need recruits; and besides, it was impossible to convert a normal adult human being into an Adapted Man—pantropy had to begin before conception, as it had been begun with Sweeney.

Calamitously, the reverse also appeared to be true. Sweeney had been unable to find anybody in the colony who believed it possible to convert an Adapted Man back into a human being. The promise the Port cops had held out to him—though they had never made it directly—thus far appeared to be founded upon nothing better than dust. If it were nevertheless possible to bring a man like Sweeney back to life, only Rullman knew about it, and Sweeney had to be hypercautious in questioning Rullman. The scientist had already made some uncomfortable deductions from the sparse facts and ample lies with which Sweeney had, by order of the Port cops, provided him. Like everyone else on Ganymede, Sweeney had learned to respect the determination and courage which were bodied forth in everything Rullman did and said; but unlike anybody else on Ganymede, he feared Rullman's understanding.

And in the meantime—while Sweeney waited, with a fatalism disturbed only by Mike Leverault, for Rullman to see through him to the other side of the gouge which was Sweeney's frigid tangled substitute for a human soul—there remained the question of the crime.

We must have those men back. Why? *Because we need to know what they know.* Why not ask them? *They won't tell us.* Why not? *Because they're afraid.* What of? *They committed a crime and must be punished.* What did they do?

SILENCE

So the question of the crime still remained. It had not been commerce-raiding; even had the Ganymedians achieved the impossible and had pirated spacecraft, that would not have been the *first* crime, the one which had made the Adapted Men flee to Ganymede in the first place, the crime from which the whole technique of pantropy had sprung. What high crime had the parents of the Adapted Men committed, to force them to maroon their children on Ganymede for what they must have believed was to be forever?

The responsibility was not the children's, that much was also obvious. The children had never been on the Earth at all. They had been born and raised on the Moon, in strict secrecy. The cops' pretense that the colonists themselves were wanted back for some old evil was another fraud, like the story about commerce-raiding. If a crime had been committed on Earth, it had been committed by the normal Earthmen whose frigid children roamed Ganymede now; it could have been committed by no-one else.

Except, of course, by Rullman. Both on the Moon and on Ganymede it was the common assumption that Rullman had been an Earth-normal human being once. That was impossible, but it was agreed to be so. Rullman himself turned the question away rather than deny it. Perhaps the crime had been his alone, since there was nobody else who could have committed it.

But *what* crime? Nobody on Ganymede could, or would, tell Sweeney. None of the colonists believed in it. Most of them thought that nothing was held against them but their difference from normal human beings; the exceptional few thought that the development of pantropy itself was the essential crime. Of that, clearly, Rullman was guilty, if "guilty" was the applicable word.

Why pantropy, or the responsibility for developing it, should be considered criminal was a mystery to Sweeney, but

26

there was a great deal else that he didn't know about Earth laws and standards, so he wasted no more time in puzzling over it. If Earth said that inventing or using pantropy was a crime, that was what it was; and the Port cops had already told him that he must not fail to bring back Rullman, no matter how grievously he failed to fulfill all his other instructions. It was an answer, and that was enough.

But why hadn't the cops said so in the first place? And why, if pantropy was a crime, had the cops themselves compounded that identical crime—by creating Sweeney?

Belatedly, he quickened his pace. Mike had already disappeared under the lowering brow of the great cavern. He could not remember noticing, now, which of the dozen smaller entrances she had used, and he himself did not know where more than two of them led. He chose one at random.

Four turns later, he was hopelessly lost.

This was unusual, but it was not entirely unexpected. The network of tunnels under Howe's *pi* was a labyrinth, not only in fact but by intention. In drilling out their home, the Adapted Men had taken into consideration the possibility that gun-carrying men in spacesuits might some day come looking for them. Such a man would never find his way out from under the mountain, unless an Adapted Man who had memorized the maze led him out; and he would never find an Adapted Man, either. Memorization was the only key, for no maps of the maze existed, and the colonists had a strictly enforced law against drawing one.

Sweeney had perhaps half of the maze committed to memory. If he did not meet someone he knew—for after all, nobody was hiding from *him*—he could count upon entering a familiar section sooner or later. In the meantime, he was curious to see anything that there was to be seen.

The first thing of interest that he saw was Dr. Rullman. The scientist emerged from a tunnel set at a 20° angle to the one Sweeney was in at the moment, going away from Sweeney and unaware of him. After an instant's hesitation, Sweeney followed him, as silently as possible. The noisy ventilation system helped to cover his footfalls.

Rullman had a habit of vanishing for periods ranging from half a day to a week. Anybody who knew where he went and what he did there did not talk about it. Now was a chance, perhaps, for Sweeney to find out for himself. It was possible, of course, that Rullman's disappearances were related to the forthcoming meteorological crisis on Ganymede, about which Sweeney had been hearing an increasing number of hints. On the other hand . . . what was on the other hand? There could be no harm in investigating.

Rullman walked rapidly, his chin ducked into his chest, as though he were travelling a route so familiar that habit could be entrusted with carrying him along it. Once Sweeney almost lost him, and thereafter cautiously closed up the interval between them a little; the labyrinth was sufficiently complex to offer plenty of quick refuges should Rullman show signs of turning back. As the scientist moved, there came from him an unpredictable but patterned series of wordless sounds, intoned rather than spoken. They communicated nothing, actuated no mechanisms, gave Rullman no safe-conduct—as was evidenced by the fact that Sweeney was travelling the same course without making any such noise. Indeed, Rullman himself seemed to be unaware that he was making it.

Sweeney was puzzled. He had never heard anybody hum before.

The rock beneath Sweeney's feet began to slope downward, gently but definitely. At the same time, he noticed that the air was markedly warmer, and was becoming more so with almost every step. A dim sound of laboring machinery was pulsing in it.

It got hotter, and still hotter, but Rullman did not hesitate. The noise—which Sweeney could now identify definitely as that of pumps, many of them—also increased. The two men were now walking down a long, straight corridor, bordered by closed doors rather than maze exits; it was badly lit, but Sweeney nevertheless allowed Rullman to get farther ahead of him. Toward the other end of this corridor, the heat began to diminish, to Sweeney's relief, for he had begun to feel quite dizzy. Rullman gave no indication that he even noticed it.

At this end Rullman ducked abruptly into a side entrance which turned out to be the top of a flight of stone steps. Quite a perceptible draft of warm air was blowing down it. Warm air, Sweeney knew, was supposed to rise in a gravitational field; why it should be going in the opposite direction he could not imagine, especially since there appeared to be no blowers in operation on this level. Since it was blowing toward Rullman, it would also carry any noise Sweeney made ahead of him. He tiptoed cautiously down.

Rullman was not in sight when Sweeney left the stairwell. There was before Sweeney, instead, a long, high-ceilinged passageway which curved gently to the right until vision was cut off. Along the inside of the curve, regularly spaced, were crouching machines, each one with a bank of laterally-coiled metal tubing rearing before it. These were the sources of the sounds Sweeney had heard.

Here, it was cold again; abnormally cold, despite the heavy current of warm air blowing down the stairwell. Something, Sweeney thought, was radically wrong with the behaviour of the thermody-namic laws down here.

He slouched cautiously ahead. After only a few steps, past the first of the laboring mechanisms—yes, it was coldest by the shining coils, as if cold were actually radiating from them —he found an undeniable airlock. Furthermore, it was in use: the outer door was sealed, but a little light beside it said that the lock was cycling. Opposite the lock, on the other wall, one of a row of spacesuit lockers hung open and tenantless.

But it was the legend painted on the airlock valve which finally made everything fall into place. It said:

PANTROPE LABORATORY ONE
Danger — Keep Out!

Sweeney dodged away from the airlock with a flash of pure panic, as a man wanted for murder might jump upon seeing a sign saying "50,000 volts." It was all clear now. There was nothing wrong with the thermodynamics of this corridor that was not similarly "wrong" inside any refrigerator. The huge engines were pumps, all right—heat pumps. Their coils were frost-free only because there was no water vapor in Ganymede's air; nevertheless, they were taking heat from that air and transferring it to the other side of that rock wall, into the pantrobe lab.

No wonder the laboratory was sealed off from the rest of the maze by an airlock—and that Rullman had had to put on a spacesuit to go through it.

It was hot on the other side. Too hot for an Adapted Man. But *what* Adapted Man?

What good was pantropy to Rullman here? That phase of history was supposed to be over and done with. Yet what was going on in this laboratory obviously was as alien to the environment of Ganymede as Ganymede's environment was to Earth's.

A is to B as B is to—what? To C? Or *to* A?

Was Rullman, in the face of the impossibility of such a project, *trying to re-adapt his people to Earth?*

There should be dials or meters on this side of the wall which would give more information as to what it was like on the other side. And there they were, in a little hooded embrasure which Sweeney had overlooked in the first shock. They said:

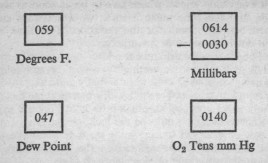

059		—	0614
			0030
Degrees F.			Millibars

047		0140
Dew Point		O_2 Tens mm Hg

Some of these meant nothing to Sweeney: he had never before encountered pressure expressed in millibars, let alone the shorthand way it was registered on the meter before him; nor did he know how to compute relative humidity from the dew point. With the Fahrenheit scale he was vaguely familiar, vaguely enough to have forgotten how to convert it into Centigrade readings. But—

Oxygen tension!

There was one planet, and one only, where such a measurement could have any meaning.

Sweeney ran.

He was no longer running by the time he had reached Rullman's office, although he was still thoroughly out of breath. Knowing that he would be unable to cross back over the top of the pantrobe lab again, feeling that heat beating up at him and knowing at least in part what it meant, he had gone in the opposite direction, past the gigantic heat-exchangers, and blundered his way up from the other side. The route he had followed had covered over three erratic miles, and several additional discoveries which had shaken him almost as hard as had the first one.

He was entirely unsure that he was even rational any more. But he had to know. Nothing was important to him now but the answer to the main question, the permanent founding or dashing of the hope under which he had lived so long.

Rullman was already back in the office, almost surrounded by his staff. Sweeney pushed his way forward among the Ganymedians, his jaw set, his diaphragm laboring.

"This time we're going to close all the safety doors," Rullman said into the phone. "The pressure fronts are going to be too steep to allow us to rely on the outside locks alone. See to it that everybody knows where he's to be as soon as the alert sounds, and this time make it stick; we don't want anybody trapped between doors for the duration. This time it may swoop down on us at damn short notice."

The phone murmured and cut out.

"Hallam, how's the harvesting? You've got less than a week, you know."

"Yes, Dr. Rullman—we'll be through in time."

"And another thing—oh, hello, Donald. What's the matter? You're looking a little pasty. I'm pretty busy, so make it fast, please."

"I'll make it fast," Sweeney said. "I can put it all into one question if I can talk to you privately. For just a few seconds."

Rullman's reddish eyebrows went up, but after examining Sweeney's face more closely, the scientist nodded and rose. "Come next door, then. . . . Now then, youngster, spit it out. With the storm coming up, we don't have time for shilly-shallying."

"All right," Sweeney said, taking a long breath. "This is it: Is it possible to change an Adapted Man back into a human being? An Earth-normal human being?"

Rullman's eyes narrowed very slowly; and for what seemed a long time, he said nothing. Sweeney looked back. He was afraid, but he was no longer afraid of Rullman.

"You've been down below, I see," the scientist said at last, drumming at the base of his chin with two fingers. "And from the terms you use, it strikes me that Shirley Leverault's educational methods left—well, the cliché springs to mind—something to be desired. But we'll let those things pass for now.

"The answer to your question, in any case, is: *No.* You will never be able to live a normal life in any other place than Ganymede, Donald. And I'll tell you something else that your mother should have told you: You ought to be damned glad of it."

"Why should I?" Sweeney said, almost emotionlessly.

"Because, like every other person in this colony, you have a Jay-positive blood type. This wasn't concealed from you when we found it, on the first day you joined us, but evidently it didn't register—or had no special significance for you. Jay-positive blood doesn't mean anything on Ganymede, true enough. *But Jay-positive Earth-normal people are cancer-*

prones. They are as susceptible to cancer as hemophiliacs are to bleeding to death—and upon equally short notice.

"If by some miracle you *should* be changed to an Earth-normal man, Donald, you would be under immediate sentence of death. So I say you should be glad that it can't happen—damn glad!"

3

The crisis on Ganymede—though of course it would not even be an incident, were there nobody there to live through it—comes to fruition roughly every eleven years and nine months. It is at the end of this period that Jupiter—and hence his fifteen-fold family of moons and moonlets—makes his closest approach to the Sun.

The eccentricity of Jupiter's orbit is only 0.0484, which amounts to very little for an ellipse which averages 483,300,-000 miles from its focal points. Nevertheless, at perihelion Jupiter is nearly ten million miles closer to the Sun than he is at aphelion; and the weather on Jupiter, never anything less than hellish, becomes indescribable during that approach. So, on a smaller but sufficient scale, does the weather on Ganymede.

The perihelion temperature on Ganymede never rises high enough to melt the ice of Neptune's Trident, but it does lift through the few niggardly degrees necessary to make the vapor pressure of Ice III known in Ganymede's air. Nobody on Earth could dream of calling the resulting condition "humidity," but Ganymede's weather turns upon such microscopic changes; an atmosphere containing *no* water will react rapidly to even a fractional vapor content. For one thing, it will pick up more heat. The resulting cycle does not go through more than a few turns before it flattens out, but the end-product is no less vicious.

The colony, Sweeney gathered, had come through one such period without any but minor difficulties, simply by withdrawing entirely under the mountain; but for many reasons that course was no longer possible. There were now semi-permanent installations—weather stations, observatories, radio beacons, bench-marks and other surveying monuments—which could be dismantled only with the loss of much time before the crisis, and re-established with still more loss afterwards.

Furthermore, some of them would be needed to report and record the progress of the crisis itself, and hence had to stay where they were.

"And don't get the idea," Rullman told a mass meeting of the colonists, gathered in the biggest cavern of the maze, "that even the mountain can protect us all the way through this one. I've told you before, but I'll remind you again, that the climax this year coincides with the peak of the sunspot cycle. Everybody's seen what that does to the weather on Jupiter proper. We can expect similar effects, to scale, on Ganymede. There's going to be trouble no matter how well we prepare. All we can hope for is that the inevitable damage will be minor. Anybody who thinks we're going to get off scot-free has only to listen for a minute."

In the calculated, dramatic pause which followed, everybody listened. The wind was audible even down here, howling over the outlets and intakes of the ventilation system, carried, amplified and encrusted with innumerable echoes, by the metal miles of the air ducts. The noise was a reminder that, at the height of the coming storm, the exterior ports would all be closed, so that everyone under the mountain would have to breathe the recirculated air. After a moment, a mass sigh—an involuntary intake of breath against the easily imagined future—passed through Rullman's audience. He grinned.

"I don't mean to frighten you," he said. "We'll get along. But I don't want any complacency either, and above all, I won't stand for any sloppiness in the preparations. It's particularly important that we keep the outside installations intact this time, because we're going to need them before the end of the next Jovian year—a long time before that, if everything continues to go well."

The grin was suddenly quenched. "I don't need to tell some of you how important it is that we get that project completed on schedule," Rullman said, quietly. "We may not have much time left before the Port cops decide to move in on us—it amazes me that they haven't already done so, particularly since we're harboring a fugitive the cops troubled to chase almost into our atmosphere—and we can't plan on their giving us any leeway.

"For those of you who know about the project only in outline, let me emphasize that there is a good deal more hanging from it than immediately meets the eye. Man's whole future in space may be determined by how well we carry it off; we can't afford to be licked—neither by the Earth nor by the weather. If we are, our whole long struggle for survival will

33

have been meaningless. I'm counting on everyone here to see to it that that doesn't happen."

It was difficult to be sure of what Rullman was talking about when he got onto the subject of the "project." It had something to do with the pantrope labs, that much was clear; and it had to do also with the colony's original spaceship, which Sweeney had run across that same day, stored in a launching chimney almost identical with the one on the Moon out of which Sweeney had been rocketed to begin his own free life, and fitted—if judgment based upon a single brief look could be trusted—either for a long voyage by a few people, or for a short trip by a large group.

Beyond that, Sweeney knew nothing about the "project," except for one additional fact of which he could make nothing: it had something to do with the colony's long-term arrangements for circumventing the loss of unfixed genes. Possibly—nobody would be less able to assess the possibility than Sweeney—the only connection this fact had with the "project" was that it *was* long-term.

Sweeney, in any event, knew better than to ask questions. The storm that was going on inside him took precedence, anyhow; as far as he was concerned, it was even more important than the storms that were sweeping Ganymede, or any that might sweep that world in the foreseeable future. He was not used to thinking in terms of a society, even a small one; Rullman's appeals to that Ideal were simply incomprehensible to him. He was the solar system's most thorough-going individualist—not by nature, but by design.

Perhaps Rullman sensed it. Whether he did or not, the assignment he gave Sweeney might have been perfectly calculated to throw a lonely man into the ultimate isolation he feared; to put the burden of an agonizing decision entirely upon the shoulders of the man who had to carry it; or—to isolate a Port spy where he could do the least harm while the colony's attention was fully occupied elsewhere. Or possibly, even probably, he had none of these motives in mind; what counted, in any event, was what he did.

He assigned Sweeney to the South polar weather station, for the duration of the emergency.

There was almost nothing to do there but watch the crystals of methane "snow" bank against the windows, and keep the station tight. The instruments reported back to base by themselves, and needed no further attention. At the height of the crisis, perhaps, Sweeney might find himself busy for a while; or, he might not. That remained to be seen.

In the meantime, he had plenty of time to ask questions—

and nobody to ask them of but himself, and the hooting, constantly rising wind.

There was an interlude. Sweeney hiked, on foot, back to Howe's H to recover the radio transceiver he had buried there, and then hiked back to the weather station. It took him eleven days, and efforts and privations of which Jack London might have made a whole novel. To Sweeney it meant nothing; he did not know whether or not he would want to use the radio after he got back with it; and as for the saga of his solo journey, he did not know that it was a saga, or even that it had been unusually difficult and painful. He had nothing against which to compare it, not even fiction; he had never read any. He measured things by the changes they made in his situation, and possession of the radio had not changed the questions he was asking himself; it had only made it possible to act upon the answers, once he had any answers.

Coming back to the station, he saw a pinnah-bird. It burrowed into the nearest drift as soon as it saw him, but for the preceding instant he had had company. He never saw it again, but now and then he thought about it.

The question, put simply, was: What was he going to do now?

That he was thoroughly in love with Mike Leverault could no longer be argued. It was doubly difficult to come to grips with the emotion, however, because he did not know the name of it, and so had to reason each time with the raw experience itself, rather than with the more convenient symbol. Each time he thought about it, it shook him all over again. But there it was.

As for the colonists, he was certain that they were not criminals in any way, except by Earth's arbitary fiat. They were a hard-working, courageous, decent lot, and had offered to Sweeney the first disinterested friendliness he had ever known.

And, like all the colonists, Sweeney could not help but admire Rullman.

There, in those three propositions, rested the case against using the radio.

The time for reporting to Meiklejon was almost up. The inert transceiver on the table before Sweeney had only to send a single one of five notes, and the colony on Ganymede would be ended. The notes were coded:

WAVVY: *Have custody need pickup*
NAVVY: *Have custody need help*
VVANY: *Need custody have help*
AAVYV: *Need custody need pickup*
YYAWY: *Have custody have pickup*

What response the computer on board the ship would make, what course of action it would dictate in response to any one of those signals was unknown, but that was now almost beside the point. Any response would be inappropriate, since not one of the five signals fitted the actual situation—despite all the intellectual travail which had gone into tailoring them.

If no note were sent, Meiklejon would go away at the end of 300 days. That might mean that Rullman's "project," whatever that was, would go through—but that wouldn't save the colony. It would take Earth a minimum of two generations to breed and mature another Sweeney from the artificially maintained ovaries of mercifully long-dead Shirley Leverault, and it was hardly likely that Earth would even try. Earth probably knew more than Sweeney did about the "project"—it would be difficult to know less—and if Sweeney himself failed to stop it, the next attempt would most likely arrive as a bomb. Earth would stop wanting "those men" back, once it became evident that she couldn't get them even through so subtle a double agent as Sweeney.

Item: chain reaction. There was, Sweeney knew, a considerable amount of deuterium on Ganymede, some of it locked in the icy wastes of Neptune's Trident, a lesser amount scattered through the rocks in the form of lithium deuteride. A fission bomb going off here would stand an excellent chance of starting a fusion explosion which would detonate the whole satellite. If any still-active fragment of that explosion should hit Jupiter, only a bare 665,000 miles away now, that planet would be quite large enough to sustain a Bethé or carbon cycle; it was diffuse, but it alone among the planets had the mass. The wave front of *that* unimaginable catastrophe would boil Earth's seas in their beds; it might also—the probability was about ⅜—trigger a nova outburst from the Sun, though nobody would stay alive to be grateful very long if it didn't.

Since Sweeney knew this, he had to assume that it was common knowledge, and that Earth would use chemical explosives only on Ganymede. But would it? Common knowledge and Sweeney had had precious little contact so far.

Still, it hardly mattered. If Earth bombed the colony, it would be all up with him, regardless. Even the limited companionship, the wordless love, the sense that he might yet be born, all would be gone. He would be gone. So might the little world.

But if he signalled Meiklejon and the computer, he would be taken alive away from Mike, away from Rullman, away from the colony, away and away. He would stay his own dead self. He might even have a new chance to learn that same endless lesson about the shapes loneliness can take; or, Earth might work a miracle and turn him into a live, Jay-positive human being.

The wind rose and rose. The congruent furies of the storms inside and outside Sweeney mounted together. Their congruence made a classic example, had he been able to recognize it, of the literary device called "the pathetic fallacy"—but Sweeney had never read any fiction, and recognizing nature in the process of imitating art would have been of no use to him anyhow.

He did not even know that, when the crisis of the exterior storm began to wear away the windward edge of the weather station's foundations with a million teeth of invisible wrath, his lonely battle to save the station might have made an epic. Whole chapters, whole cantos, whole acts of what might have been conscious heroism in another man, in a human being, were thrown away while Sweeney went about his business, his mind on his lonely debate.

There was no signal he could send that would tell Meiklejon or the computer the truth. He did not have custody of the men Earth wanted, and he didn't want to have it, so it would be idiotic to ask for help to get it. He no longer believed that Earth "must have those men back," either for Earth's purposes—mysterious though they remained—or for his own, essentially hopeless though his own appeared to be.

But any signal would take him off Ganymede—if he wanted to be taken.

The crisis, he saw, was over. He made the station fast.

He checked the radio once more. It worked. He snapped the turning pointer to one of its copper contacts and closed the key, sending Meiklejon VVANY. After half an hour, the set's oscillator began to peep rhythmically, indicating that Meiklejon was still in Ganymede's sky, and had heard.

Sweeney left the set on the table in the station, went back to the mountain, and told Rullman what he was and what he had done.

Rullman's fury was completely quiet, and a thousand times more frightening than the most uncontrolled rage could have been. He simply sat behind his desk and looked at Sweeney, all the kindness gone out of his face, and the warmth out of his eyes. After a few moments, Sweeney realized that the blankness of Rullman's eyes meant that he was not seeing him at all; his mind was turned inward. So was his rage.

"I'm astonished," he said, in a voice so even that it seemed to contain no surprise at all. "Most of all, I'm astonished at myself. I should have anticipated something like this. But I didn't dream that they had the knowledge, or the guile, to stake everything on a long-term program like this. I have been, in short, an idiot."

His voice took on, for a moment, a shade of color, but it was so scathing that it made Sweeney recoil. And yet no single word of condemnation of Sweeney had yet been forthcoming from Rullman; the man was, instead, strafing himself. Sweeney said tentatively:

"How could you have known? There were a lot of points where I might have given myself away, but I was doing my damndest not to. I might have kept the secret still longer, if I'd wanted it that way."

"You?" Rullman said. The single syllable was worse than a blow. "You're as blameless as a machine, Donald. I know too much about pantropy to think otherwise. It's very easy to isolate an Adapted infant, prevent him from becoming a human being at all, if you've sufficient ill-will to want to. Your behavior was predictable, after all."

"Was it?" Sweeney said, a little grimly. "I came and told you, didn't I?"

"And what if you did? Can that change matters now? I'm sure that Earth included that very high probability in its plans. Insofar as you have loyalties at all, they were bound to become divided; but it was probably calculated that they would stay divided—that is, would not change completely. And so here you are, trying to play both ends against the middle—you yourself being the middle—by betraying your masquerade to me at the same time you betray the colony to Earth. Nothing can be accomplished by that."

"Are you sure?"

"Quite sure," Rullman said stonily. "I suppose they offered you an inducement. Judging by the questions you've asked me before, they must have promised to make an Earth-normal human being out of you—as soon as they found out from us how to do that. But the fact of the matter is that it can't be done at all, and you know it. And now there's no future for you with us, either. I'm sorry for you, Donald, believe me; it's not your fault that they made you into a creature instead of a person. But you are nothing now but a bomb that's already gone off."

Sweeney had never known his father, and the hegemony of the Port cops had been too diffuse to instill in him any focussed, automatic respect for persons standing *in loco par-*

entis. He discovered, suddenly, that he was furious with Rullman.

"That's a silly damn speech," he said, staring down and across the desk at the seated, slightly bowed man. "Nothing's gone off yet. There's plenty of information I can give you that you might use, if you want to work to get it. Of course if you've given up in advance—"

Rullman looked up. "What do you know?" he said, with some puzzlement. "You said yourself that it would be the computer on board this Capt. Meiklejon's ship that would decide the course of action. And you can't communicate effectively with Meiklejon. This is a strange time to be bluffing, Donald."

"Why would I bluff? I know more about what Earth is *likely* to do with my message than anybody else in the colony. My experience with Earth is more recent. I wouldn't have come to you at all if I'd thought the situation to be hopeless—and if I hadn't carefully picked the one message to send to Meiklejon that I thought left the colony some hope. I'm not straddling. I'm on your side. To send no message at all would have been the worst possible thing to do. This way, we may have a grace period."

"And just how," Rullman said slowly, "can you expect me to trust you?"

"That's your problem," Sweeney said brusquely. "If I really am still straddling, it's because the colony's failed to convince me that my future lies here. And if that's the case, I'm not alone—and it's the colony's own fault for being so secretive with its own people."

"Secretive?" Rullman said, with open astonishment now. "About what?"

"About the 'project.' About the original crime Earth wants you for. About why Earth wants you back—you in particular, Dr. Rullman."

"But—that's common knowledge, Donald. All of it."

"Maybe so. But it isn't common to *me*—and most of the original settlers take it all so much for granted that they can't talk about it, except in little cryptic references, like a private joke everybody's supposed to know. But everybody doesn't; did you know that? I've found that about half your second generation here has only the foggiest notion of the past. The amount of information available here to a newcomer—whether he's newly arrived like me, or just plain newborn—you could stick in a pinnah-bird's eye. And that's dangerous. It's why I could have betrayed the colony *completely* if I hadn't decided against it, and you couldn't have stopped me."

Rullman leaned back and was quiet for quite a long time.

"Children often don't ask questions when they think they're already expected to know the answers," he murmured. He looked considerably more thunderstruck than he had when Sweeney made his original announcement. "They like to appear knowing even when they aren't. It gives them status in their own eyes."

"Children and spies," Sweeney said. "There are certain questions neither of them can ask, and for almost the same reasons. And the phonier the children's knowledge actually is, the easier for the spy to get around among the adults."

"I begin to see," Rullman said. "We thought we were immune to spying, because an Earth spy couldn't live here without elaborate, detectable protections. But that was a problem in physics, and that kind of problem is soluble. We should have assumed so from the beginning. Instead, we made ourselves socially as vulnerable as possible."

"That's how I see it. I'll bet that my father wouldn't have let you get away with it if he'd been able to get away with you. He was supposed to have been an expert in that kind of thing. I don't know; I never knew him. And I suppose it's beside the point, anyhow."

"No," Rullman said. "It's very much to the point, and I think you've just proven it, Donald. Your father couldn't prevent it, but perhaps he's given us an instrument for repairing it."

"Meaning me?"

"Yes. Ringer or no ringer, the blood you carry—and the genes—have been with us from the beginning, and I know how they show their effects. I see them now. Sit down, Donald. I begin to hope. What shall we do?"

"First of all," Sweeney said, "please, please tell me what this colony is all about!"

It was a difficult assignment.

Item: the Authorities. Long before space travel, big cities in the United States had fallen so far behind any possibility of controlling their own traffic problems as to make purely political solutions chimerical. No city administration could spend the amount of money needed for a radical cure, without being ousted in the next elections by the enraged drivers and pedestrians who most needed the help.

Increasingly, the traffic problems were turned over, with gratitude and many privileges, to semi-public Port, Bridge and Highway Authorities: huge capital-investment ventures modelled upon the Port of New York Authority, which had shown its ability to build and/or run such huge operations as the Holland and Lincoln Tunnels, the George Washington Bridge, Teterboro, LaGuardia, Idlewild and Newark airports, and many lesser facilities. By 1960 it was possible to travel from the tip of Florida to the border of Maine entirely over Authority-owned territory, if one could pay the appropriate tolls (and didn't mind being shot at in the Poconos by embattled land-owners who were still resisting the gigantic Incadel project).

Item: the tolls. The Authorities were creations of the states, usually acting in pairs, and as such enjoyed legal protections not available to other private firms engaged in interstate commerce. Among these protections, in the typical enabling act, was a provision that "the two said states will not . . . diminish or impair the power of the Authority to establish, levy and collect tolls and other charges . . ." The federal government helped; although the Federal Bridge Act of 1946 required that the collection of tolls must cease with the payment of amortization, Congress almost never invoked the Act against any Authority. Consequently, the tolls never dropped; by 1953 the Port of New York Authority was reporting a profit of over twenty million dollars a year, and annual collections were increasing at the rate of ten per cent a year.

Some of the take went into the development of new facilities—most of them so placed as to increase the take, rather than solve the traffic problem. Again the Port of New York Authority led the way; it built, against all sense, a third tube for the Lincoln Tunnel, thus pouring eight and a half million more cars per year into Manhattan's mid-town area, where the city was already strangling for want of any adequate ducts to take away the then-current traffic.

Item: the Port cops. The Authorities had been authorized from the beginning to police their own premises. As the Authorities got bigger, so did the private police forces.

By the time space travel arrived, the Authorities owned it. They had taken pains to see that it fell to them; they had learned from their airport operations—which, almost alone among their projects, always showed a loss—that nothing less than total control is good enough. And characteristically, they never took any interest in any form of space-travel which did not involve enormous expenditures; otherwise they could take no profits from sub-contracting, no profits from fast amortization of loans, no profits from the laws allowing them fast tax write-offs for new construction, no profits from the indefinitely protracted collection of tolls and fees after the initial cost and the upkeep had been recovered.

At the world's first commercial spaceport, Port Earth, it cost ship owners $5000 each and every time their ships touched the ground. Landing fees had been outlawed in private atmosphere flying for years, but the Greater Earth Port Authority operated under its own set of precedents; it made landing fees for spacecraft routine. And it maintained the first Port police force which was bigger than the armed forces of the nation which had given it its franchise; after a while, the distinction was wiped out, and the Port cops *were* the armed forces of the United States. It was not difficult to do, since the Greater Earth Port Authority was actually a holding company embracing every other Authority in the country, including Port Earth.

And when people, soon after spaceflight, began to ask each other, "How shall we colonize the planets?," the Greater Earth Port Authority had its answer ready.

Item: terraforming.

Terraforming—remaking the planets into near-images of the Earth, so that Earth-normal people could live on them. Port Earth was prepared to start small. Port Earth wanted to move Mars out of its orbit to a point somewhat closer to the sun, and make the minor adjustments needed in the orbits of the other planets; to transport to Mars about enough water to empty the Indian Ocean—only a pittance to Earth, after all, and not 10 per cent of what would be needed later to terraform Venus; to carry to the little planet-top-soil about equal in area to the state of Iowa, in order to get started at growing plants which would slowly change the atmosphere of Mars; and so on. The whole thing, Port Earth pointed out reasonably, was perfectly feasible from the point of view of the available supplies and energy resources, and it would cost less than thirty-three billion dollars. The Greater Earth Port Authority was prepared to recover that sum at no cost in taxes in less than a century, through such items as $50 rocket-mail stamps, $10,000 Mars landing fees, $1,000 one-way strap-down tickets, 100-per-desert-acre land titles, and so on. Of course the fees would continue after the cost was recovered—for maintenance.

And what, after all, the Authority asked reasonably, was the alternative? Nothing but domes. The Greater Earth Port Authority hated domes. They cost too little to begin with, and the volume of traffic to and from them would always be miniscule. Experience on the Moon had made that painfully clear. And the public hated domes, too; it had already shown a mass reluctance to live under them.

As for the governments, other than that of the United

States, that the Authority still tolerated, none of them had any love for domes, or for the kind of limited colonization that the domes stood for. They needed to get rid of their pullulating masses by the bucket-full, not by the eye-dropper-full. If the Authority knew that emigration increases the home population rather than cuts it, the Authority carefully refrained from saying so to the governments involved; they could rediscover Franklin's Law for themselves. Domes were out; terraforming was in.

Then came pantropy.

If this third alternative to the problem of colonizing the planets had come as a surprise to the Authority, and to Port Earth, they had nobody to blame for it but themselves. There had been plenty of harbingers. The notion of modifying the human stock genetically to live on the planets as they were found, rather than changing the planets to accommodate the people, had been old with Olaf Stapledon; it had been touched upon by many later writers; it went back, in essence, as far as Proteus, and as deep into the human mind as the werewolf, the vampire, the fairy changeling, the transmigrated soul.

But suddenly it was possible; and, not very long afterwards, it was a fact.

The Authority hated it. Pantropy involved a high initial investment to produce the first colonists, but it was a method which with refinement would become cheaper and cheaper. Once the colonists were planted, it required no investment at all; the colonists were comfortable on their adopted world, and could produce new colonists without outside help. Pantropy, furthermore, was at its *most* expensive less than half as costly as the setting-up of the smallest and least difficult dome. Compared to the cost of terraforming even so favorable a planet as Mars, it cost nothing at all, from the Authority's point of view.

And there was no way to collect tolls against even the initial expense. It was too cheap to bother with.

WILL YOUR CHILD BE A MONSTER?

If a number of influential scientists have their way, some child or grandchild of yours may eke out his life in the frozen wastes of Pluto, where even the sun is only a spark in the sky—and will be unable to return to Earth until after he dies, *if then!*

Yes, even now there are plans afoot to change innocent unborn children into alien creatures who would die terribly the moment that they set foot upon the green planet of their ancestors. Impatient with the slow but steady pace of man's conquest of Mars, prominent ivory-tower thinkers are working out ways to produce all kinds of travesties upon the human form—travesties which will be able to survive, somehow, in the bitterest and most untamed of planetary infernos.

The process which may produce these pitiful freaks—at enormous expense—is called "pantropy." It is already in imperfect and dangerous existence. Chief among its prophets is white-haired, dreamy-eyed Dr. Jacob Rullman, who . . .

"Stop," Sweeney said.

He put his fingertips to his temples, and then, trembling, took them away again and looked at Rullman. The scientist put down the old magazine clipping, which even in its telfon sheath was as yellow as *paella* after its half-life in Ganymede's air. Rullman's own hands were quite steady; and what there was left of his hair was as reddish-brown as ever.

"Those lies!—I'm sorry. But they work, I know they work. That's what they filled me up with. It's different when you realize how vicious they are."

"I know," Rullman said, gently. "It's easy to do. Bringing up an Adapted child is a special process, the child is always isolated and anxious to imitate, you may tell it anything you wish; it has no choice but to believe, it's desperate for closer contact, for acceptance, for the embraces it can never have. It's the ultimate in bottle-babies: the breast that might have fed it may be just on the other side of the glass, but it also lies generations in the past. Even the voice of the mother comes along a wire—if it comes along at all. I know, Donald, believe me. It happened to me, too. And it's very hard."

"Jacob Rullman was—"

"My remote, immediate father. My mother died early. They often do, of the deprivation, I believe; like yours. But my father taught me the truth, there in the Moon caves, before he was killed."

Sweeney took a deep breath. "I'm learning all that now. Go on."

"Are you sure, Donald?"

"Go on. I need to know, and it's not too late. Please."

"Well," Rullman said reflectively, "the Authority got laws passed against pantropy, but for a while the laws didn't have many teeth; Congress was leary of forbidding vivisection at the same time, and didn't know exactly what it *was* being asked to forbid; Port didn't want to be too explicit. My father was determined to see pantropy tried while the laws still provided some loopholes—he knew well enough that they'd be stiffened as soon as Port thought it safe to stiffen them. And he was convinced that we'd never colonize the stars by dome-building or terraforming. Those might work on some of our local planets—Mars, Venus—but not outside."

"Outside? How would anybody get there?"

"With the interstellar drive, Donald. It's been in existence for decades, in fact for nearly half a century. Several exploratory voyages were made with it right after it was discovered, all of them highly successful—though you'll find no mention of them in the press of the time. Port couldn't see any profit emerging out of interstellar flight and suppressed the news, sequestered the patents, destroyed the records of the trips—insofar as it could. But all the Port ships have the overdrive, just in case. Even our ship has it. So does your ferry-pilot friend up there."

Sweeney shut up.

"The thing is this: most planets, even right here inside the solar system, won't sustain domes to begin with, and can't be terraformed in any even imaginable way. Jupiter, for instance. And too many others will yield to either procedure too slowly, and too unprofitably, to tempt Port. Over interstellar distances, Port won't even try, since there'd be no trade or traffic it could collect against.

"Pantropy was the obvious answer—not for Port, certainly, but for man's future in general. Somehow, my father sold that idea to some politicians, and to some people with money, too. He was even able to find several survivors of those early interstellar expeditions, people who knew some of the extra-solar planets *and* the operation of the overdrive. All these people wanted to make at least one demonstration experiment in pantropy, an open-ended one which would lead to others if it succeeded.

"We are that experiment: this colony on Ganymede.

"Port had it outlawed before it was fairly started, but by the time they found the Moon labs it was too late; we got away. It was then that they put teeth into the laws, and made them retroactive; they had to kill pantropy, and they knew it.

"And that is why our very existence is a crime, Donald. And it is an absolute requirement of Port's policy that the colony be a failure, and that they *be able to prove it*. That's why they want us back. They want to be able to exhibit us, to show what helpless freaks we are on Earth, and to tell their people that we couldn't get along on Ganymede either, and had to be bailed out of our own mess.

"After that—well, there are those phony commerce-raiding charges you told me about. We'll be tried. We'll be executed, most likely, by exposing us in public to Earth-normal conditions. It would be a fine object-lesson; indeed, the finishing touch."

Sweeney crouched down in his chair, utterly revolted by the first complete emotion he had ever experienced: loathing for himself. He understood, now, the overtones in Rullman's voice. Everyone had been betrayed—everyone!

The voice went on without mercy, piling up the ashes. "Now, as for the project, our project that is, that's equally as simple. We know that in the long run human beings can't colonize the stars without pantropy. We know that Port won't allow pantropy to be used. And we know, therefore, that we ourselves have to carry pantropy to the stars, before Port can head us off. One, two, three, infinity.

"So that's what we're going to do, or *were* going to do. We've got our old ship fitted out for the trip, and we've got a new generation of children—just a small number—trained to operate it, and adapted for—well, for someplace. The kids can't live on Earth, and they can't live on Ganymede; but they can live on one of six different extra-solar planets we've picked out—each one of which is at a different compass-point, and at a different distance from Sol. I know the names of only two of them, the kids are the only ones who know the rest. Which one they'll actually go to will be decided only after they're aloft and on their way. Nobody who stays behind will be able to betray them. Earth will never find them.

"There will be the beginning of the most immense 'seeding program' in man's history: seeding the stars with people.

"*If* we can still manage to get it off the ground."

In the silence that followed, the door of Rullman's office opened quietly, and Mike Leverault came in, looking preoccupied and carrying a clipboard. She stopped when she saw them, and Sweeney's heart constricted on the thawing slush inside its stiffly pumping chambers.

"Excuse me," she said. "I thought . . . Is there something wrong? You both look so grim—"

"There's something wrong," Rullman said. He looked at Sweeney.

A corner of Sweeney's mouth twitched, without his willing it. He wondered if he were trying to smile, and if so, about what.

"There's no help for it," he said. "Dr. Rullman, your colonists will have to revolt against you."

4

The starshell burst high, perhaps three miles up. Though it was over the western edge of the plateau, enough light spilled down to the floor of the Gouge to checker the rocking, growling halftrack.

The sound, however, was too faint to break through the noise of the turbines, and Sweeney wasn't worried about the brief light. The truck, pushing its way north at a good twenty miles an hour beneath the wild growth, would be as difficult to detect from the air as a mouse running among roots.

Besides, nobody would be likely to be looking into the Gouge now. The evidences of battle sweeping the highlands were too compelling; Sweeney himself was following them tensely.

Mike was doing the driving, leaving Sweeney free to crouch in the tool- and instrument-littered tonneau by the big aluminum keg, watching the radar screen. The paraboloid basketwork of the radar antenna atop the truck was not sweeping; it was pointing straight back along the way he and Mike had come, picking up a microwave relay from the last automatic station that they had passed. The sweeping was being done for Sweeney, by the big radio-telescope atop Howe's *pi*.

Sweeney paid little attention to the near, low, fast streaks on the screen. They were painted there by rocket ordnance of low calibre—a part of the fighting which had no bearing on the overall pattern. That pattern was already clear: it showed, as it had for days, that the insurgent forces still held the mountain and its heavy weapons, but that the attacking salient from the loyalists' camp up north was maintaining the initiative, and was gathering strength.

It had developed into a running stalemate. Though the insurgents had obviously managed to drive the loyalists out of Howe's *pi*, perhaps by some trick with the ventilators, perhaps by some form of guerrilla warfare, they were equally evidently no match for the loyalists in the field. There they were losing ground twice as fast as they had originally taken it. The supporting fire from the mountain didn't seem to be helping them much; it was heavy, but it was terribly inaccurate. The frequent starshells told their own story of bad visibility and worse intelligence. And the loyalists, ousted though they were, had all the planes; they had the effrontery to fly them over the lines with riding lights.

What the loyalists would do when confronted with the problem of retaking the mountain was another question. Nothing short of very heavy stuff would make much of a dent on Howe's *pi*. And, even overlooking the fact that the heavy stuff was all inside the mountain, it would be suicide for *either* force to use it on Ganymede. The fighting hadn't become that bitter, yet. But it yet might.

And the Earth ships that showed on the screen inside the halftrack knew it. That much showed clearly by their disposition. They were there, almost surely, because they had deduced that Sweeney was leading the insurgents—but they showed no desire to draw in and give Sweeney a hand. Instead, they stood off, a little inside the orbit of Callisto, about 900,000 miles from Ganymede—far enough to give themselves a good running start if they saw an atomic spark on Ganymede, close enough to bail Sweeney out once it seemed that he had gained the victory anyhow.

Mike's voice, shouting something unintelligible, came back to him mixed in with the roaring of the halftrack's turbines.

"What's the matter?" he shouted, cocking his head.

". . . that rock-tumble ahead. If it's as . . . before . . . probably break the beam."

"Stop her," Sweeney shouted. "Want another reading."

The halftrack halted obediently, and Sweeney checked his screen against Rullman's readings, which showed on tumblers snicking over on a counter near his elbow. It checked; 900,-000 was close enough. Maybe a little closer, but not much. The wave-front of a full satellary explosion would cross that distance in about five seconds, carrying instant obliteration with it; but five seconds would be long enough to allow the automatics on the Earth ships to slam them away on transfinite drive.

He slapped her on the shoulder, twice. "Okay so far. Go ahead."

Her reply was lost, but he saw her crash-helmet nod, and the truck began to cant itself slowly and crazily up a long, helter-skelter causeway of boulders and rubble: a sort of talus-slope, one of many rolled each year into the Gouge by exfoliation in the cliffs. Mike turned and smiled back at him gleefully, and he smiled back; the treads were clanking too loudly to permit any other answer.

The whole scheme had depended from the beginning upon so long a chain of *ifs* that it could still fall apart at any moment and at any flawed link. It had been dependable only at

48

the beginning. The signal Sweeney had sent Meiklejon—
VVANY—had told Meiklejon nothing, since he didn't know
the code; but it had told the computer that Sweeney still
lacked custody of the Adapted Men that Earth wanted, but
that he had the help he thought he would need in getting that
custody eventually. That much was a known. What orders
the computer would rap out for Meiklejon in response com-
prised the first of the *ifs*.

The computer might, of course, react with some incredibly
bold piece of gamemanship too remote from normal human
thinking to be even guessable; Shannon's chess-playing machines sometimes won games from masters that way, though
more usually they could barely hold their own against dubs.
Since there was no way to anticipate what such a gambit
would be like, neither Sweeney nor Rullman had wasted any
time trying to pretend that there was.

But the other alternative was much more likely. The machine would assume that Sweeney was safe, as was evidenced
by the arrival of the coded signal; and that if he had help he
could only have gathered about him a secret core of disaf-
fected colonists, a "Loyal Ganymedian Underground" or
equivalent. Earth would assume, and would build the assumption into the computer, that many of the colonists were dis-
satisfied with their lives; it was a hope that Earth could turn
into a fact without being aware of the delusion, since nobody
on Earth could suspect how beautiful Ganymede was. And
the computer would assume, too, that it might be only a matter of time before Sweeney also had custody, and would be
sending Meiklejon WAVVY—or maybe even YYAWY.

"How will we know if it does?" Rullman had demanded.

"If it does, then the deadline will pass without Meiklejon's
making a move. He'll just stick to his orbit until the computer
changes his mind. What else could it tell him to do, anyhow?
He's just one man in a small ship without heavy armament.
And he's an Earthman at that—he couldn't come down here
and join my supposed underground group even if the idea occurred to him. He'll sit tight."

The halftrack heaved itself over an almost cubical boulder,
slid sidewise along its tilted face, and dropped heavily to the
bed of smaller rounded stones. Sweeney looked up from the
radar controls to see how the big aluminum keg was taking
the ride. It was awash in a sea of hand tools—picks, adzes,
sledges, spikes, coils of line rapidly unwinding—but it was se-
curely strapped down. The miracle of fireworks chemistry
(and specifically, Ganymedian chemistry) still slumbered in-

side it. He clambered forward into the cab beside Mike and strapped himself down to enjoy the ride.

There was no way to predict or to calculate how long an extension of the deadline the machine on Meiklejon's ship would allow Sweeney for the launching of his insurrection. The colony worked as though there would be no grace period at all. When the deadline passed without any sign that Meiklejon even existed—though the radio-telescope showed that he was still there—Sweeney and Rullman did not congratulate each other. They could not be sure that the silence and the delay meant what they had every good reason to hope that it meant. They could only go on working.

The movements of machines, men, and energy displays which should look to Meiklejon like a revolt of the colonists burst away from Howe's *pi* eleven days later. All the signs showed that it had been the loyalists who had set up their base near the north pole of Ganymede. Sweeney and Mike had driven through the Gouge before, for that purpose, planting in a radar-crazy jungle a whole series of small devices, all automatic, all designed to register on Meiklejon's detectors as a vast bustle of heavy machinery. The visible stragetic movements of the opposing armies had suggested the same loyalist concentration at the pole.

And now Sweeney and Mike were on their way back.

The computer appeared to be waiting it out; Meiklejon had evidently fed the data to it as a real rebellion. Sweeney's side obviously was carrying the field at first. The computer had no reason to run a new extrapolation up to the first day the loyalist forces had managed to hold their lines; and then it had to run squarely up against the question of how the loyalists could take the mountain even if, in the succeeding weeks, they should sweep the field clear of Sweeney.

"Kid stuff," Sweeney had said. "It hasn't any reason to think differently. Too simple to make it extrapolate beyond the first derivative."

"You're very confident, Donald."

Sweeney stirred uneasily in the bucket seat as he recalled Rullman's smile. No Adapted Man, least of all Sweeney, had had any real childhood; no "kid stuff." Fortunately the Port cops had thought it essential to Sweeney's task that he know theory of games.

The halftrack settled down to relatively smooth progress once more, and Sweeney got up to check the screen. The talus-slope, as Mike had anticipated, cut off reception from the radar relay station behind them; Sweeney started the antenna sweeping. Much of the field was cropped by the near edge of the Gouge, but that effect would begin to disappear gradually from the screen now. The floor of the Gouge rose steadily as one approached the north pole, although it never quite reached the level of the plains. He could already capture enough sky to be satisfied that the Earth ships were just where they had been before.

That had been the last risk: that Meiklejon, alarmed at the computer's continued counsels of inaction, would radio Earth for advice from higher authorities. Obviously a colonists' revolt on Ganymede, one that could be painted as a "We want to go home" movement, would be ideal for Earth's purposes. Earth would not only insist on Meiklejon's sitting tight as his computer had told him to do—but would also hasten to bring up reinforcements for Sweeney, just in case.

Both Sweeney and Rullman had known how likely that was to happen, and had decided to take the chance, and make preparations against it. The chance had not paid off—the Earth ships were here—but it still looked as though the preparations might.

As content as was possible under the circumstances, Sweeney went forward. Before reaching for his safety belt, he stopped to kiss Mike, to the considerable detriment of her control of the lurching truck.

The explosion threw him, hard, halfway across the empty bucket seat.

He struggled up, his head ringing. The truck's engines seemed to have stopped; beneath the ringing, he could hear nothing but the sound of the blowers.

"Don! Are you all right? What was that?"

"Ugh," he said, sitting down. "Nothing broken. Hit my head a crack. It was high explosive, from the sound. A big one."

Her face was pinched and anxious in the soft glow from the dashboard. "One of ours? Or—"

"I don't know, Mike. Sounded like it hit back down the ravine a distance. What's the matter with the engine?"

She touched the starter. It whined, and the engine caught at once. "I must have stalled it," she said apologetically. She put it in gear. "But it doesn't feel right. The traction's bad on your side."

Sweeney swung the cab door open and dropped to the stony ground. Then he whistled.

"What is it?"

"That was closer than I thought," he called back. "The righthand track is cut almost in half. A flying rock splinter, I suppose. Toss me the torch."

She leaned far out across his seat, reaching the arc-cutter to him, and then the goggles. He made his way to the rear of the truck and snapped the switch. The electric arc burned sulfur-blue; a moment later, the damaged track was unwinding from around the four big snowmobile tires like an expiring snake. Dragging the cord behind him, Sweeney cut the left track off, too, and then returned to the cab, rewinding the cord as he went.

"Okay, but take it slow. Those tires are going to be cut to ribbons by the time we hit that base."

Her face was still white, but she asked no more questions. The halftrack began to crawl forward, a halftrack no longer. At a little over two miles farther on, the first of the eight tires blew, making them both jump. A hasty check showed that it was the right outside rear one. Another two and a half miles, and the right inside drive tire blew out, too. It was bad to have two gone on the same side of the truck, but at least they were on different axles and in alternate position. The next one to go, five miles farther on—the ground became less littered as it rose—was the left inside rear.

"Don."

"Yes, Mike."

"Do you think that was an Earth bomb?"

"I don't know, Mike. I doubt it; they're too far away to be throwing stuff at Ganymede except at random, and why would they do that? More likely it was one of our torpedoes, out of control." He snapped his fingers. "Wait a minute. If we're throwing H.E. at each other, now, the cops will have noticed, and *that* we can check."

Bang!

The halftrack settled down to the right and began to slobber at the ground. No check was needed to tell Sweeney that that one had been the right outside driver. Those two wheels would be hitting on bare rims within the next thousand feet or so of travel; the main weight of the vehicle was back there —the steering tires took very little punishment, comparatively.

Gritting his teeth, he unbuckled the safety and scrambled back to the radar set, checking the aluminum drum automatically as he went.

There was much more sky showing on the screen now. It was impossible to triangulate the positions of the Earth ships now that the transmission from Howe's *pi* was cut off, but the pips on the screen were markedly dimmer. Sweeney guessed that they had retreated at least another hundred thousand miles. He grinned and leaned into Mike's ear.

"It was one of ours," he said. "Rullman's stepping up on the heavy artillery, that's all. One of his torpedo pilots must have lost one in the Gouge. The Port cops have detected the step-up, all right—they've backed off. It's beginning to look more and more as though the rebels might try to smear the loyalist base with a fission bomb, and they don't want to be cheek to cheek with the planet when that happens. How far do we have to go, still?"

Mike said, "We're—"

Bang! Mike grabbed for the switch, and the engine died.

"—here," she finished, and then, amazingly, began to giggle.

Sweeney swallowed, and then discovered that he was grinning, too. "With three track-tires intact," he said. "Hooray for us. Let's get on the job."

Another starshell broke open in the sky, not as near as before. Sweeney went around to the back of the truck, Mike picking her way after him, both of them looking ruefully at the wreathes of shredded silicone rubber which once had been two excellent tires. Two of the rims were quite bare; the fifth deflated tire, which had not been driven on, was only a puncture and might be salvaged.

"Unstrap the barrel and roll 'er out the tailgate," Sweeney said. "Easy. Now let's lower 'er to the ground, and over there."

All around them, concealed among the rocks and the massive, gnarled trunks, were the little instruments whose busy electronic chattering made this spot sound like a major military encampment to the ships lying off Ganymede. Photographs, of course, would not be expected to show it: the visible light was insufficient, the infra-red still weaker, and ultraviolet plates would be stopped by the atmosphere. Nobody would expect to *see* anything from space by any method, not in the Gouge; but the detectors would report power being expended, and power sources moving about—and rebel torpedoes homing purposefully on the area. That should be enough.

With Mike's help, Sweeney stood the aluminum barrel on end roughly in the center of this assemblage. "I'm going to take that punctured tire off," he said. "We've got fifteen minutes until take-off time, and we may need it later. Know how to wire up this thing?"

"I'm not an idiot. Go change your tire."

While Sweeney worked, Mike located the main input lead for the little invisible chatterers and spliced a line into it. To this she rigged a spring-driven switch which would snap to "Off" as soon as current was delivered to a solenoid which actuated its trigger. One strand of reel-wound cable went to the solenoid, another to a red-splashed terminal on the side of the aluminum keg. She checked the thumb-plunger at the other end of the cable. Everything was ready. When that plunger was pushed, the little chatterers would go Off, at the same moment that the barrel went On.

"All set, Mike?"

"Ready and waiting. Five minutes until take-off time."

"Good," Sweeney said, taking the reel from her. "You'd better get in the truck and take it on across the pole—over the horizon from here."

"Why? There's no real danger. And if there is, what good would I be over there alone?"

"Look, Mike," Sweeney said. He was already walking backwards, still to the north, paying out cable. "I just want to get that truck out of here; maybe we can use it, and once that barrel starts, it just might set the truck on fire. Besides, supposing the cops decide to take a close look down here? The truck's visible, or at least it's suspiciously regular. But they couldn't see *me*. It'd be far better to have the truck over the horizon. Fair enough?"

"Oh, all right. Just don't get yourself killed, that's all."

"I won't. I'll be along after the show's over. Go on, beat it."

Scowling, though not very convincingly, she climbed back into the truck, which pulled slowly away up the grade. Sweeney could hear its bare rims screeching against upthrusts of rock long after it had disappeared, but finally it was out of earshot as well.

He continued to walk backward, unwinding the cable from the reel until it was all gone, and the phony encampment was a full mile south of him. He took the thumb switch in his right hand, checked his watch, and crouched down behind a long low spur to wait.

A whole series of starshells made a train of blue suns across the sky. Somewhere a missile screamed, and then the ground shook heavily. Sweeney fervently hoped that the "insurgent" torpedomen weren't shaving it too fine.

But it wouldn't be long now. In just a few seconds, the survival ship—the ship aimed at one of six unknown stars, and carrying the new generation of Adapted children—would take off from Howe's *pi*.

Twenty seconds.

Fifteen.

Ten.

Nine.

Eight.

Seven.

Six.

Sweeney pushed the plunger.

The aluminum keg ignited with a hollow cough, and an intense ball of light, far too bright to be shut out either by the welding goggles or by closed eyelids or by both, rose into Ganymede's sky. The heat struck against Sweeney's skin as strongly as the backwash of the JATO unit had done, so long ago. The concussion, which followed about nine seconds later, flattened him and made his nose bleed.

Uncaring, he rolled over and looked upward. The light had already almost died. There was now a roiling column of white smoke, shot through with lurid, incandescent colors, hurling itself skyward at close to a mile a minute.

It was altogether a hell of a convincing-looking fission bomb—for a fake.

The column didn't begin to mushroom until it was almost five miles high, but by that time Sweeney was sure that there wasn't an Earth ship anywhere within ten astronomical units of Ganymede. Nobody would stop to make inquiries, especially when all the instruments in the "encampment" had stopped transmitting simultaneouly with the "blast."

It might perhaps occur to Port later that the "blast" might have been a huge, single-shot Roman candle fired from an aluminum keg, propelled by a mixture of smoke-flare compounds and low-grade chemical explosives. But by that time, the survival ship would be gone beyond all possibility of tracing its path.

As a matter of fact, it was gone already. It had left on the count, uncounted by Sweeney, of Zero.

Sweeney got up, humming cheerfully—and quite as tunelessly as Rullman—and continued to plod north. On the other side of the pole, the Gouge was supposed to continue to become shallower as it proceeded into the Jupiter-ward hemisphere of Ganymede. There was a twilight zone there, illuminated by the sun irregularly because of libration while Ganymede was on the sunward side of Jupiter, and quite regularly as the satellite went toward and away from occultation with the big primary. Of course the occultation periods would be rather cold, but they lasted less than eight hours apiece.

Elsewhere on Ganymede, the other colonists were heading for similar spots, their spurious war equipment destroyed, their purpose fulfilled. They were equipped variously, but all as well as Sweeney; and he had a sound ten-wheeled snowmobile, on which the six remaining tires could be redistributed to make the vehicle suitable for heavy tractoring, and with a tonneau loaded with tools, seeds, slips and cuttings, medical supplies, reserve food and fuel. He also had a wife.

Earth would visit Ganymede, of course. But it would find nothing. The inside of Howe's *pi* had been razed when the survival ship had taken off. As for the people, they would be harmless, ignorant, and *widely* scattered.

Peasants, Sweeney thought. Whistling, he crossed the north pole. Nothing but peasants.

At last he saw the squat shape of the truck, crouched at the mouth of a valley. At first Mike was not visible, but finally he spotted her, standing with her back to him on a rise. He clambered up beside her.

The valley was narrow for about a hundred feet ahead, and then it opened out in a broad fan of level land. A faint haze hovered over it. To an Earthman, nothing could have looked more desolate—but no Earthman was looking at it.

"I'll bet that's the best farm land on Ganymede," Sweeney whispered. "I wish—"

Mike turned and looked at him. He cut the wish off unspoken, but there was no doubt that Mike had fathomed it. But Rullman was no longer on Ganymede to share its beauties—this one, or any other. Though he would never see the end of the journey, and could not have survived at its goal, he had gone with the children on the ship—and taken his exportable knowledge with him.

He had been, Sweeney knew, a great man. Greater, perhaps, than his father.

"Go on ahead with the truck, Mike," Sweeney said softly. "I'll walk on behind you."

"Why? It'll ride easy on that soil—the extra weight won't matter."

"I'm not worrying about the weight. It's just that I want to walk it. It's—well, hell, Mike, don't you know that I'm just about to be born? Whoever heard of a kid arriving with a fourteen-ton truck?"

BOOK TWO

THE THING
IN THE ATTIC

. . . And it is written that after the Giants came to Tellura from the far stars, they abode a while, and looked upon the surface of the land, and found it wanting, and of evil omen. Therefore did they make man to live always in the air and in the sunlight, and in the light of the stars, that he would be reminded of them. And the Giants abode yet a while, and taught men to speak, and to write, and to weave, and to do many things which are needful to do, of which the writings speak. And thereafter they departed to the far stars, saying, Take this world as your own, and though we shall return, fear not, for it is yours.

—THE BOOK OF LAWS

1

Honath the Purse-Maker was haled from the nets an hour before the rest of the prisoners, as befitted his role as the arch-doubter of them all. It was not yet dawn, but his captors led him in great bounds through the endless, musky-perfumed orchid gardens, small dark shapes with crooked legs, hunched shoulders, slim hairless tails, carried, like his, in concentric spirals wound clockwise. Behind them sprang Honath on the end of a long tether, timing his leaps by theirs, since any slip would hang him summarily.

He would of course be on his way to the surface, some 250 feet below the orchid gardens, shortly after dawn in any event. But not even the arch-doubter of them all wanted to begin the trip—not even at the merciful snap-spine end of a tether —a moment before the law said, Go.

The looping, interwoven network of vines beneath them, each cable as thick through as a man's body, bellied out and down sharply as the leapers reached the edge of the fern-tree forest which surrounded the copse of horsetails. The whole party stopped before beginning the descent and looked eastward, across the dim bowl. The stars were paling more and more rapidly; only the bright constellation of the Parrot could still be picked out without doubt.

"A fine day," one of the guards said, conversationally. "Better to go below on a sunny day than in the rain, Purse-Maker."

Honath shuddered and said nothing. Of course, it was always raining down below in Hell, that much could be seen by a child. Even on sunny days, the endless pinpoint rain of transpiration, from the hundred million leaves of the eternal trees, hazed the forest air and soaked the black bog forever.

He looked around in the brightening, misty morning. The eastern horizon was black against the limb of the great red sun, which had already risen about a third of its diameter; it was almost time for the small, blue-white, furiously hot consort to follow. All the way to that brink, as to every other horizon, the woven ocean of the tree tops flowed gently in long, unbreaking waves, featureless as some smooth oil. Only nearby could the eye break that ocean into its details, into the world as it was: a great, many-tiered network, thickly overgrown with small ferns, with air-drinking orchids, with a thousand varieties of fungi sprouting wherever vine crossed vine and collected a little humus for them, with the vivid parasites sucking sap from the vines, the trees, and even each other. In the ponds of rainwater collected by the closely fitting leaves of the bromelaids, tree-toads and peepers stopped down their hoarse songs dubiously as the light grew, and fell silent one by one. In the trees below the world, the tentative morning screeches of the lizard-birds—the souls of the damned, or the devils who hunted them, no one was quite sure which—took up the concert.

A small gust of wind whipped out of the hollow above the glade of horsetails, making the network under the party shift slightly, as if in a loom. Honath gave with it easily, automatically, but one of the smaller vines toward which he had moved one furless hand hissed at him and went pouring away into the darkness beneath—a chlorophyll-green snake, come up out of the dripping aerial pathways in which it hunted in ancestral gloom, to greet the suns and dry its scales in the quiet morning. Farther below, an astonished monkey, routed out of its bed by the disgusted serpent, sprang into another tree, reeling off ten mortal insults, one after the other, while still in mid-leap. The snake, of course, paid no attention, since it did not speak the language of men; but the party on the edge of the glade of horsetails snickered appreciatively.

"Bad language they favor, below," another of the guards said. "A fit place for you and your blasphemers, Purse-Maker. Come now."

The tether at Honath's neck twitched, and then his captors were soaring in zig-zag bounds down into the hollow toward the Judgment Seat. He followed, since he had no choice, the tether threatening constantly to foul his arms, legs, or tail, and—worse, far worse—making his every movement mortally ungraceful. Above, the Parrot's starry plumes flickered and faded into the general blue.

Toward the center of the saucer above the grove, the stitched leaf-and-leather houses clustered thickly, bound to the vines themselves, or hanging from an occasional branch too high or too slender to bear the vines. Many of these purses Honath knew well, not only as visitor but as artisan. The finest of them, the inverted flowers which opened automatically as the morning dew bathed them, yet which could be closed tightly and safely around their occupants at dusk by a single draw-string, were his own design as well as his own handiwork. They had been widely admired and imitated.

The reputation that they had given him, too, had helped to bring him to the end of the snap-spine tether. They had given weight to his words among others—weight enough to make him, at last, the arch-doubter, the man who leads the young into blasphemy, the man who questions the Book of Laws.

And they had probably helped to win him his passage on the Elevator to Hell.

The purses were already opening as the party swung among them. Here and there, sleepy faces blinked out from amid the exfoliating sections, criss-crossed by relaxing lengths of dew-soaked rawhide. Some of the awakening householders recognized Honath, of that he was sure, but none came out to follow the party—though the villagers should be beginning to drop from the hearts of their stitched flowers like ripe seed-pods by this hour of any normal day.

A Judgment was at hand, and they knew it—and even those who had slept the night in one of Honath's finest houses would not speak for him now. Everyone knew, after all, that Honath did not believe in the Giants.

Honath could see the Judgment Seat itself now, a slung chair of woven cane crowned along the back with a row of gigantic mottled orchids. These had supposedly been transplanted there when the chair was made, but no one could remember how old they were; since there were no seasons, there was no particular reason why they should not have been there forever. The Seat itself was at the back of the arena and high above it, but in the gathering light Honath could make out the white-furred face of the Tribal Spokesman, like a lone silver-and-black pansy among the huge vivid blooms.

At the center of the arena proper was the Elevator itself. Honath had seen it often enough, and had himself witnessed Judgments where it was called into use, but he could still hardly believe that he was almost surely to be its next passenger. It consisted of nothing more than a large basket, deep enough so that one would have to leap out of it, and rimmed with thorns to prevent one from leaping back in. Three hempen ropes were tied to its rim, and were then cunningly interwound on a single-drum windlass of wood, which could be turned by two men even when the basket was loaded.

The procedure was equally simple. The condemned man was forced into the basket, and the basket lowered out of sight, until the slackening of the ropes indicated that it had touched the surface. The victim climbed out—and if he did not, the basket remained below until he starved or until Hell otherwise took care of its own—and the windlass was rewound.

The sentences were for varying periods of time according to the severity of the crime, but in practical terms this formality was empty. Although the basket was dutifully lowered when the sentence had expired, no one had ever been known to get back into it. Of course, in a world without seasons or moons, and hence without any but an arbitrary year, long periods of time are not easy to count accurately. The basket may often have arrived thirty or forty days to one side or the other of the proper date. This was only a technicality, however, for if keeping time was difficult in the attic world, it was probably impossible in Hell.

Honath's guards tied the free end of his tether to a branch and settled down around him. One abstractedly passed a pine cone to him, and he tried to occupy his mind with the business of picking the juicy seeds from it, but somehow they had no flavor.

More captives were being brought in now, while the Spokesman watched with glittering black eyes from his high perch. There was Mathild the Forager, shivering as if with ague, the fur down her left side glistening and spiky, as though she had inadvertently overturned a tank plant on herself. After her was brought Alaskon the Navigator, a middle-aged man only a few years younger than Honath himself; he was tied up next to Honath, where he settled down at once, chewing at a joint of cane with apparent indifference.

Thus far, the gathering had proceeded without more than a few words being spoken, but that ended when the guards tried to bring Seth the Needlesmith from the nets. He could be heard at once, over the entire distance to the glade, alternately chattering and shrieking in a mixture of tones that might mean fear or fury. Everyone in the glade but Alaskon turned to look, and heads emerged from purses like new butterflies from cocoons.

A moment later, Seth's guards came over the lip of the glade in a tangled group, now shouting themselves. Somewhere in the middle of the knot Seth's voice became still louder; obviously he was clinging with all five members to any vine or frond he could grasp, and was no sooner pried loose from one than he would leap by main force, backwards if possible, to another. Nevertheless, he was being brought inexorably down into the arena, two feet forward, one foot back, three feet forward . . .

Honath's guards resumed picking their pine cones. During the disturbance, Honath realized, Charl the Reader had been brought in quietly from the same side of the glade. He now sat opposite Alaskon, looking apathetically down at the vine-web, his shoulders hunched forward. He exuded despair; even to look at him made Honath feel a renewed shudder.

From the high Seat, the Spokesman said: "Honath the Purse-maker, Alaskon the Navigator, Charl the Reader, Seth the Needlesmith, Mathild the Forager, you are called to answer to justice."

"Justice!" Seth shouted, springing free of his captors with a tremendous bound, and bringing up with a jerk on the end of his tether. "This is no justice! I have nothing to do with—"

The guards caught up with him and clamped brown hands firmly over his mouth. The Spokesman watched with amused malice.

"The accusations are three," the Spokesman said. "The first, the telling of lies to children. Second, the casting into doubt of the divine order among men. Third, the denial of the Book

61

of Laws. Each of you may speak in order of age. Honath the Purse-Maker, your plea may be heard."

Honath stood up, trembling a little, but feeling a surprisingly renewed surge of his old independence.

"Your charges," he said, "all rest upon the denial of the Book of Laws. I have taught nothing else that is contrary to what we all believe, and called nothing else into doubt. And I deny the charge."

The Spokesman looked down at him with disbelief. "Many men and women have said that you do not believe in the Giants, Purse-Maker," he said. "You will not win mercy by piling up more lies."

"I deny the charge," Honath insisted. "I believe in the Book of Laws as a whole, and I believe in the Giants. I have taught only that the Giants were not real in the sense that we are real. I have taught that they were intended as symbols of some higher reality, and were not meant to be taken as literal Persons."

"What higher reality is this?" the Spokesman demanded. "Describe it."

"You ask me to do something the writers of the Book of Laws themselves couldn't do," Honath said hotly. "If they had to embody the reality in symbols rather than writing it down directly, how could a mere pursemaker do better?"

"This doctrine is wind," the Spokesman said. "And it is plainly intended to undercut authority and the order established by the Book. Tell me, Purse-Maker, if man need not fear the Giants, why should they fear the law?"

"Because they are men, and it is to their interest to fear the law. They aren't children, who need some physical Giant sitting over them with a whip to make them behave. Furthermore, Spokesman, this archaic belief *itself* undermines us. As long as we believe that there are real Giants, and that some day they'll return and resume teaching us, so long will we fail to seek answers to our questions for ourselves. Half of what we know was given to us in the Book, and the other half is supposed to drop to us from the skies if we wait long enough. In the meantime, we vegetate."

"If a part of the Book be untrue, there can be nothing to prevent that it is all untrue," the Spokesman said heavily. "And we will lose even what you call the half of our knowledge—which is actually the whole of it, to those who see with clear eyes."

Suddenly, Honath lost his temper. "Lose it, then!" he shouted. "Let us unlearn everything we know only by rote, go back to the beginning, learn all over again, and continue to learn, from our own experience. Spokesman, you are an old man, but there are still some of us who haven't forgotten what curiosity means!"

"Quiet!" the Spokesman said. "We have heard enough. We call on Alaskon the Navigator."

"Much of the Book is clearly untrue," Alaskon said flatly, rising. "As a handbook of small trades it has served us well. As a guide to how the universe is made, it is nonsense, in my opinion; Honath is too kind to it. I've made no secret of what I think, and I still think it."

"And will pay for it," the Spokesman said, blinking slowly down at Alaskon. "Charl the Reader."

"Nothing," Charl said, without standing, or even looking up.

"You do not deny the charges?"

"I've nothing to say," Charl said, but then, abruptly, his head jerked up, and he glared with desperate eyes at the Spokesman. "I can read, Spokesman. I have seen words of the Book of Laws that contradict each other. I've pointed them out. They're facts, they exist on the pages. I've taught nothing, told no lies, preached no unbelief. I've pointed to the facts. That's all."

"Seth the Needlesmith, you may speak now."

The guards took their hands gratefully off Seth's mouth; they had been bitten several times in the process of keeping him quiet up to now. Seth resumed shouting at once.

"I'm no part of this group! I'm the victim of gossip, envious neighbors, smiths jealous of my skill and my custom! No man can say worse of me than that I sold needles to this pursemaker—sold them in good faith! The charges against me are lies, all of them!"

Honath jumped to his feet in fury, and then sat down again, choking back the answering shout almost without tasting its bitterness. What did it matter? Why should he bear witness against the young man? It would not help the others, and if Seth wanted to lie his way out of Hell, he might as well be given the chance.

The Spokesman was looking down at Seth with the identical expression of outraged disbelief which he had first bent upon Honath. "Who was it cut the blasphemies into the hardwood trees, by the house of Hosi the Lawgiver?" he demanded. "Sharp needles were at work there, and there are witnesses to say that your hands held them."

"More lies!"

"Needles found in your house fit the furrows, Seth."

"They were not mine—or they were stolen! I demand to be freed!"

"You will be freed," the Spokesman said coldly. There was no possible doubt as to what he meant. Seth began to weep and to shout at the same time. Hands closed over his mouth again. "Mathild the Forager, your plea may be heard."

The young woman stood up hesitantly. Her fur was nearly dry now, but she was still shivering.

"Spokesman," she said, "I saw the things which Charl the Reader showed me. I doubted, but what Honath said restored my belief. I see no harm in his teachings. They remove doubt, instead of fostering it, as you say they do. I see no evil in them, and I don't understand why this is a crime."

Honath looked over to her with new admiration. The Spokesman sighed heavily.

"I am sorry for you," he said, "but as Spokesman we cannot allow ignorance of the Law as a plea. We will be merciful to you all, however. Renounce your heresy, affirm your belief in the Book as it is written from bark to bark, and you shall be no more than cast out of the tribe."

"I renounce it!" Seth said. "I never shared it! It's all blasphemy and every word is a lie! I believe in the Book, all of it!"

"You, Needlesmith," the Spokesman said, "have lied before this Judgment, and are probably lying now. You are not included in the dispensation."

"Snake-spotted caterpillar! May your—*ummulph*."

"Purse-Maker, what is your answer?"

"It is, No," Honath said stonily. "I've spoken the truth. The truth can't be unsaid."

The Spokesman looked down at the rest of them. "As for you three, consider your answers carefully. To share the heresy means sharing the sentence. The penalty will not be lightened only because you did not invent the heresy."

There was a long silence.

Honath swallowed hard. The courage and the faith in that silence made him feel smaller and more helpless than ever. He realized suddenly that the other three would have kept that silence, even without Seth's defection to stiffen their spines. He wondered if he could have done so.

"Then we pronounce the sentence," the Spokesman said. "You are one and all condemned to one thousand days in Hell."

There was a concerted gasp from around the edges of the arena, where, without Honath's having noticed it before, a silent crowd had gathered. He did not wonder at the sound. The sentence was the longest in the history of the tribe.

Not that it really meant anything. No one had ever come

back from as little as one hundred days in Hell. No one had ever come back from Hell at all.

"Unlash the Elevator. All shall go together—and their heresy with them."

2

The basket swayed. The last of the attic world that Honath saw was a circle of faces, not too close to the gap in the vine web, peering down after them. Then the basket fell another few yards to the next turn of the windlass and the faces vanished.

Seth was weeping in the bottom of the Elevator, curled up into a tight ball, the end of his tail wrapped around his nose and eyes. No one else could make a sound, least of all Honath.

The gloom closed around them. It seemed extraordinarily still. The occasional harsh scream of a lizard-bird somehow emphasized the silence without breaking it. The light that filtered down into the long aisles between the trees seemed to be absorbed in a blue-green haze, through which the lianas wove their long curved lines. The columns of tree-trunks, the pillars of the world, stood all around them, too distant in the dim light to allow them to gauge their speed of descent; only the irregular plunges of the basket proved that it was even in motion any longer, though it swayed laterally in a complex, overlapping series of figure-eights traced on the air in response to the rotation of the planet—a Foucault pendulum ballasted with five lives.

Then the basket lurched downward once more, brought up short, and tipped sidewise, tumbling them all against the hard cane. Mathild cried out in a thin voice, and Seth uncurled almost instantly, clawing for a handhold. Another lurch, and the Elevator lay down on its side and was still.

They were in Hell.

Cautiously, Honath began to climb out, picking his way over the long thorns on the basket's rim. After a moment, Charl the Reader followed, and then Alaskon took Mathild firmly by the hand and led her out onto the surface. The footing was wet and spongy, yet not at all resilient, and it felt cold; Honath's toes curled involuntarily.

"Come on, Seth," Charl said in a hushed voice. "They

won't haul it back up until we're all out. You know that."

Alaskon looked around into the chilly mists. "Yes," he said. "And we'll need a needlesmith down here. With good tools, there's just a chance—"

Seth's eyes had been darting back and forth from one to the other. With a sudden chattering scream, he bounded out of the bottom of the basket, soaring over their heads in a long, flat leap, and struck the high knee at the base of the nearest tree, an immense fan palm. As he hit, his legs doubled under him, and almost in the same motion he seemed to rocket straight up into the murky air.

Gaping, Honath looked up after him. The young needle-smith had timed his course to the split second. He was already darting up the rope from which the Elevator was suspended. He did not even bother to look back.

After a moment, the basket tipped upright. The impact of Seth's weight hitting the rope evidently had been taken by the windlass team to mean that the condemned people were all out on the surface; a twitch on the rope was the usual signal. The basket began to rise, bobbing and dancing. Its speed of ascent, added to Seth's, took his racing dwindling figure out of sight quickly. After a while, the basket was gone, too.

"He'll never get to the top," Mathild whispered. "It's too far, and he's going too fast. He'll lose strength and fall."

"I don't think so," Alaskon said heavily. "He's agile and strong. If anyone could make it, he could."

"They'll kill him if he does."

"Of course they will," Alaskon said, shrugging.

"I won't miss him," Honath said.

"No more will I. But we could use some sharp needles down here, Honath. Now, we'll have to plan to make our own—if we can identify the different woods, down here where there aren't any leaves to help us tell them apart."

Honath looked at the Navigator curiously. Seth's bolt for the sky had distracted him from the realization that the basket, too, was gone, but now that desolate fact hit home. "You actually plan to stay alive in Hell, don't you, Alaskon?"

"Certainly," Alaskon said calmly. "This is no more Hell than —up there—is Heaven. It's the surface of the planet, no more, no less. We can stay alive if we don't panic. Were you just going to sit here until the furies came for you, Honath?"

"I hadn't thought much about it," Honath confessed. "But if there is any chance that Seth will lose his grip on that rope —before he reaches the top and they knife him—shouldn't we wait and see if we can catch him? He can't weigh more than 35 pounds. Maybe we could contrive some sort of a net—"

"He'd just break our bones along with his," Charl said. "I'm for getting out of here as fast as possible."

"What for? Do you know a better place?"

"No, but whether this is Hell or not, there are demons down here. We've all seen them from up above, the snake-headed giants. They must know that the Elevator always lands here and empties out free food. This must be a feeding-ground for them—"

He had not quite finished speaking when the branches began to sigh and toss, far above. A gust of stinging droplets poured along the blue air, and thunder rumbled. Mathild whimpered.

"It's only a squall coming up," Honath said. But the words came out in a series of short croaks. As the wind had moved through the trees, Honath had automatically flexed his knees and put his arms out for handholds, awaiting the long wave of response to pass through the ground beneath him. But nothing happened. The surface under his feet remained stolidly where it was, flexing not a fraction of an inch in any direction. And there was nothing nearby for his hands to grasp.

He staggered, trying to compensate for the failure of the ground to move, but at the same moment another gust of wind blew through the aisles, a little stronger than the first, and calling insistently for a new adjustment of his body to the waves which passed along the treetops. Again the squashy surface beneath him refused to respond; the familiar give-and-take of the vine-web to the winds, a part of his world as accustomed as the winds themselves, was gone.

Honath was forced to sit down, feeling distinctly ill. The damp, cool earth under his furless buttocks was unpleasant, but he could not have remained standing any longer without losing his meager prisoner's breakfast. One grappling hand caught hold of the ridged, gritty stems of a clump of horsetail, but the contact failed to allay the uneasiness.

The others seemed to be bearing it no better than Honath. Mathild in particular was rocking dizzily, her lips compressed, her hands clapped to her delicate ears.

Dizziness. It was unheard of up above, except among those who had suffered grave head injuries or were otherwise very ill. But on the motionless ground of Hell, it was evidently going to be with them constantly.

Charl squatted, swallowing convulsively. "I—I can't stand," he moaned. "It's magic, Alaskon—the snake-headed demons—"

"Nonsense," Alaskon said, though he had remained standing only by clinging to the huge, mud-colored bulb of a cycadella. "It's just a disturbance of our sense of balance. It's a—motionlessness-sickness. We'll get used to it."

"We'd better," Honath said, relinquishing his grip on the horsetails by a sheer act of will. "I think Charl's right about this being a feeding-ground, Alaskon. I hear something moving around in the ferns. And if this rain lasts long, the water will rise here, too. I've seen silver flashes from down here many a time after heavy rains."

"That's right," Mathild said, her voice subdued. "The base of the ferntree grove always floods; that's why the treetops are so much lower there."

The wind seemed to have let up a little, though the rain was still falling. Alaskon stood up tentatively.

"Then let's move on," he said. "If we try to keep under cover until we get to higher ground—"

A faint crackling sound, high above his head, interrupted him. It got louder. Feeling a sudden spasm of pure fear, Honath looked up.

Nothing could be seen for an instant but the far-away curtain of branches and fern-fronds. Then, with shocking suddenness, something small and black irrupted through the blue-green roof and came tumbling toward them. It was a man, twisting and tumbling through the air with grotesque slowness, like a child turning in its sleep. They scattered.

The body hit the ground with a sodden thump, but there were sharp overtones to the sound, like the bursting of a gourd. For a moment nobody moved. Then Honath crept forward.

It had been Seth, as Honath had realized the moment the black figurine had burst through the branches far above. But it had not been the fall that had killed him. He had been run through by at least a dozen needles—some of them, beyond doubt, tools from his own shop, their points edged hair-fine by his own precious strops of leatherwood-bark, soaked until they were soft, pliant, and nearly transparent in the mud at the bottom of sun-warmed bromelaid tanks.

There would be no reprieve from above. The sentence was one thousand days. This burst and broken huddle of fur was the only alternative.

And the first day had barely begun.

They toiled all the rest of the day to reach higher ground, clinging to the earth for the most part because the trees, except for a few scattered gingkoes, flowering dogwoods and live oaks, did not begin to branch until their tunks had soared more than eighteen feet above the ground. As they stole cautiously closer to the foothills of the Great Range and the ground became firmer, they were able to take to the air for short stretches, but they were no sooner aloft among the willows than the lizard-birds came squalling down on them by the dozens, fighting among each other for the privilege of nipping these plump and incredibly slow-moving monkeys.

No man, no matter how confirmed a free-thinker, could have stood up under such an onslaught by the creatures he had been taught as a child to think of as his ancestors. The first time it happened, every member of the party dropped like a pine-cone to the sandy ground and lay paralyzed under the nearest cover, until the brindle-feathered, fan-tailed screamers tired of flying in such tight circles and headed for clearer air. Even after the lizard-birds had given up, they crouched quietly for a long time, waiting to see what greater demons might have been attracted by the commotion.

Thus far, none of the snake-headed Powers had shown themselves—though several times Honath had heard suggestively heavy movements in the jungle around them.

Luckily, on the higher ground there was much more cover available, from low-growing shrubs and trees—palmetto, sassafras, several kinds of laurel, magnolia, and a great many sedges. Up here, too, the endless jungle began to break to pour around the bases of the great pink cliffs, leaving welcome vistas of open sky, only sketchily crossed by woven bridges leading from the vine-world to the cliffs themselves. In the intervening columns of blue air a whole hierarchy of flying creatures ranked themselves, layer by layer: First the low-flying beetles, bees and two-winged insects; then the dragon-flies which hunted them, some with wingspreads as wide as two feet; then the lizard-birds, hunting the dragon-flies and anything else that could be nipped without fighting back; and at last, far above, the great gliding reptiles coasting along the brows of the cliffs, riding the rising currents of air, their long-jawed hunger stalking anything that flew—as they sometimes stalked the birds of the attic world, and the flying fish along the breast of the distant sea.

The party halted in an especially thick clump of sedges. Though the rain continued to fall, harder than ever, they were all desperately thirsty. They had yet to find a single bromelaid; evidently the tank-plants did not grow in Hell. Cupping their hands to the weeping sky accumulated surprisingly little water; and no puddles large enough to drink from accumulated on the sand. But at least, here under the open sky, there was too much fierce struggle in the air to allow the lizard-birds to congregate and squall above their hiding place.

The white sun had already set, and the red sun's vast arc still bulged above the horizon only because the light from its limb had been wrenched higher into Tellura's sky by its passage through the white sun's intense gravitational field. In the lurid glow the rain looked like blood, and the seamed faces of the pink cliffs had all but vanished. Honath peered dubiously out from under the sedges at the still-distant escarpments.

"I don't see how we can hope to climb those," he said, in a low voice. "That kind of limestone crumbles as soon as you touch it, otherwise we'd have had better luck with our war against the cliff tribe."

"We could go around the cliffs," Charl said. "The foothills of the Great Range aren't very steep. If we could last until we get to them, we could go on up into the Range itself."

"To the volcanoes?" Mathild protested. "But nothing can live up there, nothing but the white fire-things. And there are the lava-flows, too, and the choking smoke—"

"Well, we can't climb these cliffs, Honath's quite right," Alaskon said. "And we can't climb the Basalt Steppes, either —there's nothing to eat along them, let alone any water or cover. I don't see what else we can do but try to get up into the foothills."

"Can't we stay here?" Mathild said plaintively.

"No," Honath said, even more gently than he had intended. Mathild's four words were, he knew, the most dangerous words in Hell—he knew it quite surely, because of the imprisoned creature inside him that cried out to say "Yes" instead. "We have to get out of the country of the demons. And maybe—just maybe—if we can cross the great Range, we can join a tribe that hasn't heard about our being condemned to Hell. There are supposed to be tribes on the other side of the Range, but the cliff people would never let our folk get through to them. That's on our side now."

"That's true," Alaskon said, brightening a little. "And from the top of the Range, we could come *down* into another tribe —instead of trying to climb up into their village out of Hell. Honath, I think it might work."

"Then we'd better try to sleep right here and now," Charl said. "It seems safe enough. If we're going to skirt the cliffs and climb those foothills, we'll need all the strength we've got left."

Honath was about to protest, but he was suddenly too tired to care. Why not sleep it over? And if in the night they were found and taken—well, that would at least put an end to the struggle.

It was a cheerless and bone-damp bed to sleep in, but there was no better alternative. They curled up as best they could. Just before he was about to drop off at last, Honath heard Mathild whimpering to herself, and, on impulse, crawled over to her and began to smooth down her fur with his tongue. To his astonishment, each separate, silky hair was loaded with dew. Long before the girl had curled herself more tightly and her complaints had dwindled into sleepy murmurs, Honath's thirst was assuaged. He reminded himself to mention the method in the morning.

But when the white sun finally came up, there was no time to think of thirst. Charl the Reader was gone. Something had plucked him from their huddled midst as neatly as a fallen breadfruit—and had dropped his cleaned ivory skull just as negligently, some two hundred feet farther on up the slope which led toward the pink cliffs.

3

Late that afternoon, the three found the blue, turbulent stream flowing out of the foothills of the Great Range. Not even Alaskon knew quite what to make of it. It looked like water, but it flowed like the rivers of lava that crept downward from the volcanoes. Whatever else it could be, obviously it wasn't water; water stood, it never flowed. It was possible to imagine a still body of water as big as this, but only as a moment of fancy, an exaggeration derived from the known bodies of water in the tank-plants. But this much water in motion? It suggested pythons; it was probably poisonous. It did not occur to any of them to drink from it. They were afraid even to touch it, let alone cross it, for it was almost surely as hot as the other kinds of lava-rivers. They followed its course cautiously into the foothills, their throats as dry and gritty as the hollow stems of horsetails.

Except for the thirst—which was in an inverted sense their friend, insofar as it overrode the hunger—the climbing was not difficult. It was only circuitous, because of the need to stay under cover, to reconnoiter every few yards, to choose the most sheltered course rather than the most direct. By an unspoken consent, none of the three mentioned Charl, but their eyes were constantly darting from side to side, searching for a glimpse of the thing that had taken him.

That was perhaps the worst, the most terrifying part of the tragedy: that not once since they had been in Hell had they actually seen a demon, or even any animal as large as a man. The enormous, three-taloned footprint they had found in the sand beside their previous night's bed—the spot where the thing had stood, looking down at the four sleeping men from above, coldly deciding which of them to seize—was the only evidence they had that they were now really in the same world with the demons—the same demons they had sometimes looked down upon from the remote vine-webs.

The footprint—and the skull.

By nightfall, they had ascended perhaps a hundred and fifty feet. It was difficult to judge distances in the twilight, and the token vine bridges from the attic world to the pink cliffs were now cut off from sight by the intervening masses of the cliffs themselves. But there was no possibility that they could climb higher today. Although Mathild had borne the climb surprisingly well, and Honath himself still felt almost fresh, Alaskon was completely winded. He had taken a bad cut on one hip from a serrated spike of volcanic glass against which he had stumbled, and the wound, bound with leaves to prevent its leaving a spoor which might be followed, evidently was becoming steadily more painful.

Honath finally called a halt as soon as they reached the little ridge with the cave in back of it. Helping Alaskon over the last boulders, he was astonished to discover how hot the Navigator's hands were. He took him back into the cave and then came out onto the ledge again.

"He's really sick," he told Mathild in a low voice. "He needs water, and another dressing for that cut. And we've got to get both for him somehow. If we ever get to the jungle on the other side of the Range, we'll need a navigator even worse than we need a needlesmith."

"But how? I could dress the cut if I had the materials, Honath. But there's no water up here. It's a desert; we'll never get across it."

"We've got to try. I can get him water, I think. There was a big cycladella on the slope we came up, just before we passed that obsidian spur that hurt Alaskon. Gourds that size usually have a fair amount of water inside them—and I can use a piece of the spur to rip it open—"

A small hand came out of the darkness and took him tightly by the elbow. "Honath, you can't go back down there. Suppose the demon that—that took Charl is still following us? They hunt at night—and this country is all so strange . . ."

"I can find my way. I'll follow the sound of the stream of glass or whatever it is. You pull some fresh leaves for Alaskon and try to make him comfortable. Better loosen those vines around the dressing a little. I'll be back."

He touched her hand and pried it loose gently. Then, without stopping to think about it any further, he slipped off the ledge and edged toward the sound of the stream, travelling crabwise on all fours.

But he was swiftly lost. The night was thick and completely impenetrable, and he found that the noise of the stream seemed to come from all sides, providing him no guide at all. Furthermore, his memory of the ridge which led up to the cave appeared to be faulty, for he could feel it turning sharply to the right beneath him, though he remembered distinctly that it had been straight past the first side-branch, and then had gone to the left. Or had he passed the first side-branch in the dark without seeing it? He probed the darkness cautiously with one hand.

At the same instant, a brisk, staccato gust of wind came whirling up out of the night across the ridge. Instinctively, Honath shifted his weight to take up the flexing of the ground beneath him—

He realized his error instantly and tried to arrest the complex set of motions, but a habit-pattern so deeply ingrained could not be frustrated completely. Overwhelmed with vertigo, Honath grappled at the empty air with hands, feet, and tail and went toppling.

An instant later, with a familiar noise and an equally familiar cold shock that seemed to reach throughout his body, he was sitting in the midst of—

Water. Icy water, and water that rushed by him improbably with a menacing, monkeylike chattering, but water all the same.

It was all he could do to repress a hoot of hysteria. He hunkered into the stream and soaked himself. Things nibbled delicately at his calves as he bathed, but he had no reason to fear fish, small species of which often showed up in the tanks of the bromelaids. After lowering his muzzle to the rushing, invisible surface and drinking his fill, he ducked himself completely and then clambered out onto the banks, carefully neglecting to shake himself.

Getting back to the ledge was much less difficult. "Mathild," he called in a hoarse whisper. "Mathild, we've got water."

"Come in here quick then. Alaskon's worse. I'm afraid, Honath."

Dripping, Honath felt his way into the cave. "I don't have any container. I just got myself wet—you'll have to sit him up and let him lick my fur."

"I'm not sure he can."

But Alaskon could, feebly, but sufficiently. Even the coldness of the water—a totally new experience for a man who had never drunk anything but the soup-warm contents of the bromelaids—seemed to help him. He lay back at last, and said in a weak but otherwise normal voice: "So the stream was water after all."

"Yes," Honath said. "And there are fish in it, too."

"Don't talk," Mathild said. "Rest, Alaskon."

"I'm resting. Honath, if we stick to the course of the stream . . . . Where was I? Oh. We can follow the stream through the Range, now that we know it's water. How did you find that out?"

"I lost my balance and fell into it."

Alaskon chuckled. "Hell's not so bad, is it?" he said. Then he sighed, and rushes creaked under him.

"Mathild! What's the matter? Is he—did he die?"

"No . . . no. He's breathing. He's still sicker than he realizes, that's all . . . Honath—if they'd known, up above, how much courage you have—"

"I was scared white," Honath said grimly. "I'm still scared."

But her hand touched his again in the solid blackness, and after he had taken it, he felt irrationally cheerful. With Alaskon breathing so raggedly behind them, there was little chance that either of them would be able to sleep that night; but they sat silently together on the hard stone in a kind of temporary peace, and when the mouth of the cave began to outline itself, as dimly at first as the floating patches of color seen behind the closed eye, with the first glow of the red sun, they looked at each other in a conspiracy of light all their own.

Hell, Honath reflected, wasn't so bad, after all.

With the first light of the white sun, a half-grown oxyaena cub rose slowly from its crouch at the mouth of the cave, and stretched luxuriously, showing a full set of saber-like teeth. It looked at them steadily for a moment, its ears alert, then turned and loped away down the slope.

How long it had been crouched there listening to them, it was impossible to know. They had been lucky that they had stumbled into the lair of a youngster. A full-grown animal would have killed them all, within a few seconds after its cat's eyes had collected enough dawn to identify them positively. The cub, since it had no family of its own as yet, evidently had only been puzzled to find its den occupied, and uninclined to quarrel about it.

The departure of the big cat left Honath frozen, not so much frightened as simply stunned by so unexpected an end to the vigil. At the first moan from Alaskon, however, Mathild was up and walking softly to the Navigator, speaking in a low voice, sentences which made no particular sense and perhaps were not intended to. Honath stirred and followed her.

Halfway back into the cave, his foot struck something and he looked down. It was the thigh bone of some medium-large animal, imperfectly cleaned, but not very recent—possibly the keepsake the oxyaena had hoped to rescue from the usurpers of its lair. Along a curved inner surface there was a patch of thick gray mold. Honath squatted and peeled it off carefully.

"Mathild, we can put this over the wound," he said. "Some molds help prevent wounds from festering . . . How is he?"

"Better, I think," Mathild murmured. "But he's still feverish. I don't think we'll be able to move on today."

Honath was unsure whether to be pleased or disturbed. Certainly, he was far from anxious to leave the cave, where they seemed at least to be reasonably comfortable. Possibly they would also be reasonably safe, for the low-roofed hole almost surely still smelt of oxyaena, and possible intruders would recognize the smell—as the men from the attic world could not—and keep their distance. They would have no way of knowing that the cat had only been a cub to begin with, and that it had vacated the premises, though of course the odor would fade before long.

Yet it was important to move on, to cross the Great Range if possible, and in the end to win their way back to the world where they belonged; even to win vindication, no matter how long it took. Even should it prove relatively easy to survive in Hell—and there were few signs of that, thus far—the only proper course was to fight until the attic world was totally reconquered. After all, it would have been the easy and the comfortable thing, back there at the very beginning, to have kept one's incipient heresies to oneself and remained on comfortable terms with one's neighbors. But Honath had spoken up and so had the rest of them, in their fashions.

It was the ancient internal battle between what Honath wanted to do, and what he knew he ought to do. He had never heard of Kant and the Categorical Imperative, but he knew well enough which side of his nature would win in the long run. But it had been a cruel joke of heredity which had fastened a sense of duty onto a lazy nature. It made even small decisions aggressively painful.

But for the moment at least, the decision was out of his hands. Alaskon was too sick to be moved. In addition, the strong beams of sunlight which had been glaring in across the floor of the cave were dimming by the instant, and there was a distant, premonitory growl of thunder.

"Then we'll stay here," he said. "It's going to rain again, and hard this time. Once it's falling in earnest, I can go out and pick up some fruit—it'll screen me even if anything is prowling around in it. And I won't have to go as far as the stream for water, as long as the rain keeps up."

The rain, as it turned out, kept up all day, in a growing downpour which completely curtained the mouth of the cave by early afternoon. The chattering of the nearby stream grew quickly to a roar.

By evening, Alaskon's fever seemed to have dropped almost to normal, and his strength nearly returned as well. The wound, thanks more to the encrusted matte of mold than to any complications within the flesh itself, was still ugly-looking, but it was now painful only when the Navigator moved carelessly, and Mathild was convinced that it was mending. Alaskon himself, having been deprived of activity all day, was unusually talkative.

"Has it occurred to either of you," he said in the gathering gloom, "that since that stream is water, it can't possibly be coming from the Great Range? All the peaks over there are just cones of ashes and lava. We've seen young volcanoes in the process of building themselves, so we're sure of that. What's more, they're usually hot. I don't see how there could possibly be any source of water in the Range—not even run-off from the rains."

"It can't just come up out of the ground," Honath said. "It must be fed by rain. By the way it sounds now, it could even be the first part of a flood."

"As you say, it's probably rain water," Alaskon said cheerfully. "But not off the Great Range, that's out of the question. Most likely it collects on the cliffs."

"I hope you're wrong," Honath said. "The cliffs may be a little easier to climb from this side, but there's still the cliff tribe to think about."

"Maybe, maybe. But the cliffs are big. The tribes on this side may never have heard of the war with our treetop folk. No, Honath, I think that's our only course from here."

"If it is," Honath said grimly, "we're going to wish more than ever that we had some stout, sharp needles among us."

Alaskon's judgment was quickly borne out. The three left the cave at dawn the next morning, Alaskon moving somewhat stiffly but not otherwise noticeably incommoded, and resumed following the stream bed upwards—a stream now swollen by the rains to a roaring rapids. After winding its way upwards for about a mile in the general direction of the Great Range, the stream turned on itself and climbed rapidly back toward the basalt cliffs, falling toward the three over successively steeper shelves of jutting rock.

Then it turned again, at right angles, and the three found themselves at the exit of a dark gorge, little more than thirty feet high, but both narrow and long. Here the stream was almost perfectly smooth, and the thin strip of land on each side of it was covered with low shrubs. They paused and looked dubiously into the canyon. It was singularly gloomy.

"There's plenty of cover, at least," Honath said in a low voice. "But almost anything could live in a place like that."

"Nothing very big could hide in it," Alaskon pointed out. "It should be safe. Anyhow it's the only way to go."

"All right. Let's go ahead, then. But keep your head down, and be ready to jump!"

Honath lost the other two by sight as soon as they crept into the dark shrubbery, but he could hear their cautious movements nearby. Nothing else in the gorge seemed to move at all, not even the water, which flowed without a ripple over an invisible bed. There was not even any wind, for which Honath was grateful, although he had begun to develop an immunity to the motionlessness sickness.

After a few moments, Honath heard a low whistle. Creeping sidewise toward the source of the sound, he nearly bumped into Alaskon, who was crouched beneath a thickly spreading magnolia. An instant later, Mathild's face peered out of the dim greenery.

"Look," Alaskon whispered. "What do you make of this?"

"This" was a hollow in the sandy soil, about four feet across and rimmed with a low parapet of earth—evidently the same earth that had been scooped out of its center. Occupying most of it were three gray, ellipsoidal objects, smooth and featureless.

"Eggs," Mathild said wonderingly.

"Obviously. But look at the size of them! Whatever laid them must be gigantic. I think we're trespassing in something's private valley."

Mathild drew in her breath. Honath thought fast, as much to prevent panic in himself as in the girl. A sharp-edged stone lying nearby provided the answer. He seized it and struck.

The outer surface of the egg was leathery rather than brittle; it tore raggedly. Deliberately, Honath bent and put his mouth to the oozing surface.

It was excellent. The flavor was decidedly stronger than that of birds' eggs, but he was far too hungry to be squeamish. After a moment's amazement, Alaskon and Mathild attacked the other two ovoids with a will. It was the first really satisfying meal they had had in Hell. When they finally moved away from the devastated nest, Honath felt better than he had since the day he was arrested.

As they moved on down the gorge, they began again to hear the roar of water, though the stream looked as placid as ever. Here, too, they saw the first sign of active life in the valley: a flight of giant dragonflies skimming over the water. The insects took flight as soon as Honath showed himself, but quickly came back, their nearly non-existent brains already convinced that there had always been men in the valley.

The roar got louder very rapidly. When the three rounded the long, gentle turn which had cut off their view from the exit, the source of the roar came into view. It was a sheet of falling water as tall as the depth of the gorge itself, which came arcing out from between two pillars of basalt and fell to a roiling, frothing pool.

"This is as far as we go!" Alaskon said, shouting to make himself heard at all over the tumult. "We'll never be able to get up those walls!"

Stunned, Honath looked from side to side. What Alaskon had said was all too obviously true. The gorge evidently had begun life as a layer of soft, partly soluble stone in the cliffs, tilted upright by some volcanic upheaval, and then worn completely away by the rushing stream. Both cliff faces were of the harder rock, and were sheer and as smooth as if they had been polished by hand. Here and there a network of tough vines had begun to climb them, but nowhere did such a network even come close to reaching the top.

Honath turned and looked once more at the great arc of water and spray. If there were only some way to prevent their being forced to retrace their steps—

Abruptly, over the riot of the falls, there was a piercing, hissing shriek. Echoes picked it up and sounded it again and again, all the way up the battlements of the cliffs. Honath sprang straight up in the air and came down trembling, facing away from the pool.

At first he could see nothing. Then, down at the open end of the turn, there was a huge flurry of motion.

A second later, a two-legged, blue-green reptile half as tall as the gorge itself came around the turn in a single huge bound and lunged violently into the far wall of the valley. It stopped as if momentarily stunned, and the great head turned toward them a face of sinister and furious idiocy.

The shriek set the air to boiling again. Balancing itself with its heavy tail, the beast lowered its head and looked redly toward the falls.

The owner of the robbed nest had come home—and they had met a demon of Hell at last.

Honath's mind at that instant went as white and blank as the underbark of a poplar. He acted without thinking, without even knowing what he did. When thought began to creep back into his head again, the three of them were standing shivering in semi-darkness, watching the blurred shadow of the demon lurching back and forth upon the screen of shining water.

It had been nothing but luck, not foreplanning, to find that there was a considerable space between the back of the falls proper and the blind wall of the canyon. It had been luck, too, which had forced Honath to skirt the pool in order to reach the falls at all, and thus had taken them all behind the silver curtain at the point where the weight of the falling water was too low to hammer them down for good. And it had been the blindest stroke of all that the demon had charged after them directly into the pool, where the deep, boiling water had slowed the threshing hind legs enough to halt it before it went under the falls, as it had earlier blundered into the hard wall of the gorge.

Not an iota of all this had been in Honath's mind before he had discovered it to be true. At the moment that the huge reptile had screamed for the second time, he had simply grasped Mathild's hand and broken for the falls, leaping from low tree to shrub to fern faster than he had ever leapt before. He did not stop to see how well Mathild was keeping up with him, or whether or not Alaskon was following. He only ran. He might have screamed, too; he could not remember.

They stood now, all three of them, wet through, behind the curtain until the shadow of the demon faded and vanished. Finally Honath felt a hand thumping his shoulder, and turned slowly.

Speech was impossible here, but Alaskon's pointing finger was eloquent enough. Along the back wall of the falls, centuries of erosion had failed to wear away completely the original soft limestone; there was still a sort of serrated chimney there, open toward the gorge, which looked as though it could be climbed. At the top of the falls, the water shot out from between the basalt pillars in a smooth, almost solid-looking tube, arching at least six feet before beginning to break into the fan of spray and rainbows which poured down into the gorge. Once the chimney had been climbed, it should be possible to climb out from under the falls without passing through the water again.

And after that?

Abruptly, Honath grinned. He felt weak all through with reaction, and the face of the demon would probably be leering in his dreams for a long time to come—but at the same time he could not repress a surge of irrational confidence. He gestured upward jauntily, shook himself, and loped forward into the throat of the chimney.

Hardly more than an hour later they were all standing on a ledge overlooking the gorge, with the waterfall creaming over the brink next to them, only a few yards away. From here, it was evident that the gorge itself was only the bottom of a far larger cleft, a split in the pink-and-gray cliffs as sharp as though it had been driven in the rock by a bolt of sheet lightning. Beyond the basalt pillars from which the fall issued, however, the stream foamed over a long ladder of rock shelves which seemed to lead straight up into the sky. On this side of the pillars the ledge broadened into a sort of truncated mesa, as if the waters had been running at this level for centuries before striking some softer rock-stratum which had permitted them to cut down further to create the gorge. The stone platform was littered with huge rocks, rounded by long water erosion, obviously the remains of a washed-out stratum of conglomerite or a similar sedimentary layer.

Honath looked at the huge pebbles—many of them bigger than he was—and then back down into the gorge again. The figure of the demon, foreshortened into a pigmy by distance and perspective, was still roving back and forth in front of the waterfall. Having gotten the notion that prey was hiding behind the sheet of water, the creature might well stay stationed there until it starved, for all Honath knew—it certainly did not seem to be very bright—but Honath thought he had a better idea.

"Alaskon, can we hit the demon with one of these rocks?"

The navigator peered cautiously into the gorge. "It wouldn't surprise me," he said at last. "It's just pacing back and forth in that same small arc. And all things fall at the same speed;

if we can make the rock arrive just as it walks under it—hmm. Yes, I think so. Let's pick a big one to make certain."

But Alaskon's ambitions overreached his strength; the rock he selected would not move, largely because he himself was still too weak to help much with it. "Never mind," he said. "Even a small one will be falling fast by the time it gets down there. Pick one you and Mathild can roll easily yourselves; I'll just have to figure it a little closer, that's all."

After a few tests, Honath selected a rock about three times the size of his own head. It was heavy, but between them he and Mathild got it to the edge of the ledge.

"Hold on," Alaskon said in a pre-occupied voice. "Tip it over the edge, so it's ready to drop as soon as you let go of it. Good. Now wait. He's on his backtrack now. As soon as he crosses—All right. Four, three, two, one, *drop it!*"

The rock fell away. All three of them crouched in a row at the edge of the gorge. The rock dwindled, became as small as a fruit, as small as a fingernail, as small as a grain of sand. The dwarfed figure of the demon reached the end of its mad stalking arc, swung furiously to go back again—

And stopped. For an instant it just stood there. Then, with infinite slowness, it toppled sidewise into the pool. It thrashed convulsively two or three times, and then was gone; the spreading waves created by the waterfall masked any ripples it might have made in sinking.

"Like spearing fish in a bromelaid," Alaskon said proudly. But his voice was shaky. Honath knew exactly why.

After all, they had just killed a demon.

"We could do that again," Honath whispered.

"Often," Alaskon agreed, still peering greedily down at the pool. "They don't appear to have much intelligence, these demons. Given enough height, we could lure them into blind alleys like this, and bounce rocks off them almost at will. I wish *I'd* thought of it."

"Where do we go now?" Mathild said, looking toward the ladder beyond the basalt pillars. "That way?"

"Yes, and as fast as possible," Alaskon said, getting to his feet and looking upward, one hand shading his eyes. "It must be late. I don't think the light will last much longer."

"We'll have to go single file," Honath said. "And we'd better keep hold of each other's hands. One slip on those wet steps and—it's a long way down again."

Mathild shuddered and took Honath's hand convulsively. To his astonishment, the next instant she was tugging him toward the basalt pillars.

The irregular patch of deepening violet sky grew slowly as

they climbed. They paused often, clinging to the jagged escarpments until their breath came back, and snatching icy water in cupped palms from the stream that fell down the ladder beside them. There was no way to tell how far up into the dusk the way had taken them, but Honath suspected that they were already somewhat above the level of their own vine-webbed world. The air smelled colder and sharper than it ever had above the jungle.

The final cut in the cliffs through which the stream fell was another chimney, steeper and more smooth-walled than the one which had taken them out of the gorge under the waterfall, but also narrow enough to be climbed by bracing one's back against one side, and one's hands and feet against the other. The column of air inside the chimney was filled with spray, but in Hell that was too minor a discomfort to bother about.

At long last Honath heaved himself over the edge of the chimney onto flat rock, drenched and exhausted, but filled with an elation he could not suppress and did not want to. They were above the attic jungle; they had beaten Hell itself. He looked around to make sure that Mathild was safe, and then reached a hand down to Alaskon; the navigator's bad leg had been giving him trouble. Honath heaved mightily, and Alaskon came heavily over the edge and lit sprawling on the high moss.

The stars were out. For a while they simply sat and gasped for breath. Then they turned, one by one, to see where they were.

There was not a great deal to see. There was the mesa, domed with stars on all sides; a shining, finned spindle, like a gigantic minnow, pointing skyward in the center of the rocky plateau; and around the spindle, indistinct in the starlight . . .

. . . Around the shining minnow, tending it, were the Giants.

4

This, then, was the end of the battle to do what was right, whatever the odds. All the show of courage against superstition, all the black battles against Hell itself, came down to this: *The Giants were real!*

They were inarguably real. Though they were twice as tall

as men, stood straighter, had broader shoulders, were heavier across the seat and had no visible tails, their fellowship with men was clear. Even their voices, as they shouted to each other around their towering metal minnow, were the voices of men made into gods, voices as remote from those of men as the voices of men were remote from those of monkeys, yet just as clearly of the same family.

These were the Giants of the Book of Laws. They were not only real, but they had come back to Tellura as they had promised to do.

And they would know what to do with unbelievers, and with fugitives from Hell. It had all been for nothing—not only the physical struggle, but the fight to be allowed to think for oneself as well. The gods existed, literally, actually. This belief was the real hell from which Honath had been trying to fight free all his life—but now it was no longer just a belief. It was a fact, a fact that he was seeing with his own eyes.

The Giants had returned to judge their handiwork. And the first of the people they would meet would be three outcasts, three condemned and degraded criminals, three jailbreakers—the worst possible detritus of the attic world.

All this went searing through Honath's mind in less than a second, but nevertheless Alaskon's mind evidently had worked still faster. Always the most outspoken unbeliever of the entire little group of rebels, the one among them whose whole world was founded upon the existence of rational explanations for everything, his was the point of view most completely challenged by the sight before them now. With a deep, sharply indrawn breath, he turned abruptly and walked away from them.

Mathild uttered a cry of protest, which she choked off in the middle; but it was already too late. A round eye on the great silver minnow came alight, bathing them all in an oval patch of brilliance.

Honath darted after the navigator. Without looking back, Alaskon suddenly was running. For an instant longer Honath saw his figure, poised delicately against the black sky. Then he dropped silently out of sight, as suddenly and completely as if he had never been.

Alaskon had borne every hardship and every terror of the ascent from Hell with courage and even with cheerfulness—but he had been unable to face being told that it had all been meaningless.

Sick at heart, Honath turned back, shielding his eyes from

the miraculous light. There was a clear call in some unknown language from near the spindle.

Then there were footsteps, several pairs of them, coming closer.

It was time for the Second Judgment.

After a long moment, a big voice from the darkness said: "Don't be afraid. We mean you no harm. We're men, just as you are."

The language had the archaic flavor of the Book of Laws, but it was otherwise perfectly understandable. A second voice said: "What are you called?"

Honath's tongue seemed to be stuck to the roof of his mouth. While he was struggling with it, Mathild's voice came clearly from beside him:

"He is Honath the Purse-Maker, and I am Mathild the Forager."

"You are a long distance from the place we left your people," the first Giant said. "Don't you still live in the vine-webs above the jungles?"

"Lord—"

"My name is Jarl Eleven. This is Gerhardt Adler."

This seemed to stop Mathild completely. Honath could understand why: the very notion of addressing Giants by name was nearly paralyzing. But since they were already as good as cast down into Hell again, nothing could be lost by it.

"Jarl Eleven," he said, "the people still live among the vines. The floor of the jungle is forbidden. Only criminals are sent there. We are criminals."

"Oh?" Jarl Eleven said. "And you've come all the way from the surface to this mesa? Gerhardt, this is prodigious. You have no idea what the surface of this planet is like—it's a place where evolution has never managed to leave the tooth-and-nail stage. Dinosaurs from every period of the Mesozoic, primitive mammals all the way up the scale to the ancient cats—the works. That's why the original seeding team put these people in the treetops instead."

"Honath, what was your crime?" Gerhardt Adler said.

Honath was almost relieved to have the questioning come so quickly to this point; Jarl Eleven's aside, with its many terms he could not understand, had been frightening in its very meaninglessness.

"There were five of us," Honath said in a low voice. "We said we—that we did not believe in the Giants."

There was a brief silence. Then, shockingly, both Jarl Eleven and Gerhardt Adler burst into enormous laughter.

Mathild cowered, her hands over her ears. Even Honath flinched and took a step backward. Instantly, the laughter stopped, and the Giant called Jarl Eleven stepped into the oval of light and sat down beside them. In the light, it could be seen that his face and hands were hairless, although there was hair on his crown; the rest of his body was covered by a kind of cloth. Seated, he was no taller than Honath, and did not seem quite so fearsome.

"I beg your pardon," he said. "It was unkind of us to laugh, but what you said was highly unexpected. Gerhardt, come over here and squat down, so that you don't look so much like a statue of some general. Tell me, Honath, in what way did you not believe in the Giants?"

Honath could hardly believe his ears. A Giant had begged his pardon! Was this some still crueler joke? But whatever the reason, Jarl Eleven had asked him a question.

"Each of the five of us differed," he said. "I held that you were not—not real except as symbols of some abstract truth. One of us, the wisest, believed that you did not exist in any sense at all. But we all agreed that you were not gods."

"And, of course, we aren't," Jarl Eleven said. "We're men. We come from the same stock as you. We're not your rulers, but your brothers. Do you understand what I say?"

"No," Honath admitted.

"Then let me tell you about it. There are men on many worlds, Honath. They differ from one another, because the worlds differ, and different kinds of men are needed to people each one. Gerhardt and I are the kind of men who live on a world called Earth, and many other worlds like it. We are two very minor members of a huge project called a 'seeding program,' which has been going on for thousands of years now. It's the job of the seeding program to survey newly discovered worlds, and then to make men suitable to live on each new world."

"To make men? But only gods—"

"No, no. Be patient and listen," said Jarl Eleven. "We don't make men. We make them suitable. There's a great deal of difference between the two. We take the living germ plasm, the sperm and the egg, and we modify it; then the modified man emerges, and we help him to settle down in his new world. That's what we did on Tellura—it happened long ago, before Gerhardt and I were even born. Now, we've come back to see how you people are getting along, and to lend a hand if necessary."

He looked from Honath to Mathild, and back again. "Do you follow me?" he said.

"I'm trying," Honath said. "But you should go down to the jungle-top, then. We're not like the others; they are the people you want to see."

"We shall, in the morning. We just landed here. But, just because you're not like the others, we're more interested in you now. Tell me: has any condemned man ever escaped from the jungle floor before?"

"No, never. That's not surprising. There are monsters down there."

Jarl Eleven looked sidewise at the other Giant; he seemed to be smiling. "When you see the films," he remarked, "you'll call that the understatement of the century. Honath, how did you three manage to escape, then?"

Haltingly, at first, and then with more confidence as the memories came crowding vividly back, Honath told him. When he mentioned the feast at the demon's nest, Jarl Eleven again looked significantly at Adler, but he did not interrupt.

"And, finally, we got to the top of the chimney and came out on this flat space," Honath said. "Alaskon was still with us then, but when he saw you and the shining thing he threw himself back down the cleft. He was a criminal like us, but he should not have died. He was a brave man, and a wise one."

"Not wise enough to wait until all the evidence was in," Adler said enigmatically. "All in all, Jarl, I'd say 'prodigious' is the word for it. This is really the most successful seeding job any team has ever done, at least in this limb of the galaxy. And what a stroke of luck, to be on the spot just as it came to term, and with a couple at that!"

"What does it mean?" Honath said.

"Just this, Honath. When the seeding team set your people up in business on Tellura, they didn't mean for you to live forever in the treetops. They knew that, sooner or later, you'd have to come down to the ground and learn to fight this planet on its own terms. Otherwise, you'd go stale and die out."

"Live on the ground all the time?" Mathild said in a faint voice.

"Yes, Mathild. The life in the treetops was to have been only an interim period, while you gathered knowledge you needed about Tellura, and put it to use. But to be the real masters of the world, you will have to conquer the surface, too.

"The device your people worked out, of sending only criminals to the surface, was the best way of conquering the planet that they could have picked. It takes a strong will and exceptional courage to go against custom; and both those qualities

86

are needed to lick Tellura. Your people exiled just such fighting spirits to the surface, year after year after year.

"Sooner or later, some of those exiles were going to discover how to live successfully on the ground, and make it possible for the rest of your people to leave the trees. You and Honath have done just that."

"Observe please, Jarl," Adler said. "The crime in this first successful case was ideological. That was the crucial turn in the criminal policy of these people. A spirit of revolt is not quite enough; but couple it with brains, and—ecce homo!"

Honath's head was swimming. "But what does all this mean?" he said. "Are we—not condemned to Hell any more?"

"No, you're still condemned, if you still want to call it that," Jarl Eleven said soberly. "You've learned how to live down there, and you've found out something even more valuable: How to stay alive while cutting down your enemies. Do you know that you killed three demons with your bare hands, you and Mathild and Alaskon?"

"Killed—"

"Certainly," Jarl Eleven said. "You ate three eggs. That is the classical way, and indeed the only way, to wipe out monsters like the dinosaurs. You can't kill the adults with anything short of an anti-tank gun, but they're helpless in embryo—and the adults haven't the sense to guard their nests."

Honath heard, but only distantly. Even his awareness of Mathild's warmth next to him did not seem to help much.

"Then we have to go back down there," he said dully. "And this time forever."

"Yes," Jarl Eleven said, his voice gentle. "But you won't be alone, Honath. Beginning tomorrow, you'll have all your people with you."

"*All* our people? But—you're going to drive them out?"

"All of them. Oh, we won't prohibit the use of the vine-webs, too, but from now on your race will have to fight it out on the surface as well. You and Mathild have proven that it can be done. It's high time the rest of you learned, too."

"Jarl, you think too little of these young people themselves," Adler said. "Tell them what is in store for them. They are frightened."

"Of course, of course. It's obvious. Honath, you and Mathild are the only living individuals of your race who know how to survive down there on the surface. And we're not going to tell your people how to do that. We aren't even going to drop them so much as a hint. That part of it is up to you."

Honath's jaw dropped.

87

"It's up to you," Jarl Eleven repeated firmly. "We'll return you to your tribe tomorrow, and we'll tell your people that you two know the rules for successful life on the ground—and that everyone else has to go down and live there, too. We'll tell them nothing else but that. What do you think they'll do then?"

"I don't know," Honath said dazedly. "Anything could happen. They might even make us Spokesman and Spokeswoman—except that we're just common criminals."

"Uncommon pioneers, Honath. The man and woman to lead the humanity of Tellura out of the attic, into the wide world." Jarl Eleven got to his feet, the great light playing over him. Looking up after him, Honath saw that there were at least a dozen other Giants standing just outside the oval of light, listening intently to every word.

"But there's a little time to be passed before we begin," Jarl Eleven said. "Perhaps you two would like to look over our ship."

Numbly, but with a soundless emotion much like music inside him, Honath took Mathild's hand. Together they walked away from the chimney to Hell, following the footsteps of the Giants.

BOOK THREE

SURFACE TENSION

Prologue

Dr. Chatvieux took a long time over the microscope, leaving la Ventura with nothing to do but look at the dead landscape of Hydrot. Waterscape, he thought, would be a better word. From space, the new world had shown only one small, triangular continent, set amid endless ocean; and even the continent was mostly swamp.

The wreck of the seed-ship lay broken squarely across the one real spur of rock which Hydrot seemed to possess, which reared a magnificent twenty-one feet above sea-level. From this eminence, la Ventura could see forty miles to the horizon across a flat bed of mud. The red light of the star Tau Ceti, glinting upon thousands of small lakes, pools, ponds and puddles, made the watery plain look like a mosaic of onyx and ruby.

"If I were a religious man," the pilot said suddenly, "I'd call this a plain case of divine vengeance."

Chatvieux said: "Hmn?"

"It's as if we'd been struck down for—is it *hubris?* Pride, arrogance?"

"Hybris," Chatvieux said, looking up at last. "Well, is it? I don't feel swollen with pride at the moment. Do you?"

"I'm not exactly proud of my piloting," la Ventura admitted. "But that isn't quite what I mean. I was thinking about why we came here in the first place. It takes a lot of arrogance to think that you can scatter men, or at least things very much like men, all over the face of the galaxy. It takes even more pride to do the job—to pack up all the equipment and move from planet to planet and actually make men, make them suitable for every place you touch."

"I suppose it does," Chatvieux said. "But we're only one of several hundred seed-ships in this limb of the galaxy, so I doubt that the gods picked us out as special sinners." He smiled. "If they had, maybe they'd have left us our ultraphone, so the Colonization Council could hear about our cropper. Besides, Paul, we don't make men. We adapt them—adapt them to Earthlike planets, nothing more than that. We've sense enough—or humility enough, if you like that better—to know that we can't adapt men to a planet like Jupiter, or to the surface of a sun, like Tau Ceti."

"Anyhow, we're here," la Ventura said grimly. "And we aren't going to get off. Phil tells me that we don't even have our germ-cell bank any more, so we can't seed this place in the usual way. We've been thrown onto a dead world and dared to adapt to it. What are the pantropes going to do with our recalcitrant carcasses—provide built-in waterwings?"

"No," Chatvieux said calmly. "You and I and all the rest of us are going to die, Paul. Pantropic techniques don't work on the body; that was fixed for you for life when you were conceived. To attempt to rebuild it for you would only maim you. The pantropes affect only the genes, the inheritance-carrying factors. We can't give you built-in waterwings, any more than we can give you a new set of brains. I think we'll be able to populate this world with men, but we won't live to see it."

The pilot thought about it, a lump of cold blubber collecting gradually in his stomach. "How long do you give us?" he said at last.

"Who knows? A month, perhaps."

The bulkhead leading to the wrecked section of the ship was pushed back, admitting salt, muggy air, heavy with carbon dioxide. Philip Strasvogel, the communications officer, came in, tracking mud. Like la Ventura, he was now a man without a function, and it appeared to bother him. He was not well equipped for introspection, and with his ultraphone totally smashed, unresponsive to his perpetually darting hands, he had been thrown back into his own mind, whose resources were few. Only the tasks Chatvieux had set him to had prevented him from setting like a gelling colloid into a permanent state of the sulks.

90

He unbuckled from around his waist a canvas belt, into the loops of which plastic vials were stuffed like cartridges. "More samples, Doc," he said. "All alike—water, very wet. I have some quicksand in one boot, too. Find anything?"

"A good deal, Phil. Thanks. Are the others around?"

Strasvogel poked his head out and hallooed. Other voices rang out over the mudflats. Minutes later, the rest of the survivors of the crash were crowding into the pantrope deck: Saltonstall, Chatvieux' senior assistant, a perpetually sanguine, perpetually youthful technician willing to try anything once, including dying; Eunice Wagner, behind whose placid face rested the brains of the expedition's only remaining ecologist; Eleftherios Venezuelos, the always-silent delegate from the Colonization Council; and Joan Heath, a midshipman whose duties, like la Ventura's and Phil's, were now without meaning, but whose bright head and tall, deceptively indolent body shone to the pilot's eyes brighter than Tau Ceti—brighter, since the crash, even than the home sun.

Five men and two women—to colonize a planet on which "standing room" meant treading water.

They came in quietly and found seats or resting places on the deck, on the edges of tables, in corners. Joan Heath went to stand beside la Ventura. They did not look at each other, but the warmth of her shoulder beside his was all that he needed. Nothing was as bad as it seemed.

Venezuelos said: "What's the verdict, Dr. Chatvieux?"

"This place isn't dead," Chatvieux said. "There's life in the sea and in the fresh water, both. On the animal side of the ledger, evolution seems to have stopped with the crustacea; the most advanced form I've found is a tiny crayfish, from one of the local rivulets, and it doesn't seem to be well distributed. The ponds and puddles are well-stocked with small metazoans of lower orders, right up to the rotifers—including a castle-building genus like Earth's *Floscularidae*. In addition, there's a wonderfully variegated protozoan population, with a dominant ciliate type much like *Paramoecium*, plus various Sarcodines, the usual spread of phyto-flagellates, and even a phosphorescent species I wouldn't have expected to see anywhere but in salt water. As for the plants, they run from simple blue-green algae to quite advanced thallus-producing types—though none of them, of course, can live out of the water."

"The sea is about the same," Eunice said. "I've found some of the larger simple metazoans—jellyfish and so on—and some crayfish almost as big as lobsters. But it's normal to find salt-water species running larger than fresh-water. And there's the usual plankton and nannoplankton population."

"In short," Chatvieux said, "we'll survive here—if we fight."

"Wait a minute," la Ventura said. "You've just finished telling me that we wouldn't survive. And you were talking about us, the seven of us here, not about the genus man, because we don't have our germ-cells banks any more. What's—"

"We don't have the banks. But we ourselves can contribute germ-cells, Paul. I'll get to that in a moment." Chatvieux turned to Saltonstall. "Martin, what would you think of our taking to the sea? We came out of it once, long ago; maybe we could come out of it again on Hydrot."

"No good," Saltonstall said immediately. "I like the idea, but I don't think this planet ever heard of Swinburne, or Homer, either. Looking at it as a colonization problem alone, as if we weren't involved in it ourselves, I wouldn't give you an Oc dollar for *epi oinopa ponton*. The evolutionary pressure there is too high, the competition from other species is prohibitive; seeding the sea should be the last thing we attempt, not the first. The colonists wouldn't have a chance to learn a thing before they'd be gobbled up."

"Why?" la Ventura said. Once more, the death in his stomach was becoming hard to placate.

"Eunice, do your sea-going Coelenterates include anything like the Portuguese man-of-war?"

The ecologist nodded.

"There's your answer, Paul," Saltonstall said. "The sea is out. It's got to be fresh water, where the competing creatures are less formidable and there are more places to hide."

"We can't compete with a jellyfish?" la Ventura asked, swallowing.

"No, Paul," Chatvieux said. "Not with one that dangerous. The pantropes make adaptations, not gods. They take human germ-cells—in this case, our own, since our bank was wiped out in the crash—and modify them genetically toward those of creatures who can live in any reasonable environment. The result will be manlike, and intelligent. It usually shows the donors' personality patterns, too, since the modifications are usually made mostly in the morphology, not so much in the mind, of the resulting individual.

"But we can't transmit memory. The adapted man is worse than a child in the new environment. He has no history, no techniques, no precedents, not even a language. In the usual colonization project, like the Tellura affair, the seeding teams more or less take him through elementary school before they

92

leave the planet to him, but we won't survive long enough to give such instruction. We'll have to design our colonists with plenty of built-in protections and locate them in the most favorable environment possible, so that at least some of them will survive learning by experience alone."

The pilot thought about it, but nothing occurred to him which did not make the disaster seem realer and more intimate with each passing second. Joan Heath moved slightly closer to him. "One of the new creatures can have my personality pattern, but it won't be able to remember being me. Is that right?"

"That's right. In the present situation we'll probably make our colonists haploid, so that some of them, perhaps many, will have a heredity traceable to you alone. There may be just the faintest of residuums of identity—pantropy's given us some data to support the old Jungian notion of ancestral memory. But we're all going to die on Hydrot, Paul, as self-conscious persons. There's no avoiding that. Somewhere we'll leave behind people who behave as we would, think and feel as we would, but who won't remember la Ventura, or Dr. Chatvieux, or Joan Heath—or the Earth."

The pilot said nothing more. There was a gray taste in his mouth.

"Saltonstall, what would you recommend as a form?"

The pantropist pulled reflectively at his nose. "Webbed extremities, of course, with thumbs and big toes heavy and thorn-like for defense until the creature has had a chance to learn. Smaller external ears, and the eardrum larger and closer to the outer end of the ear-canal. We're going to have to reorganize the water-conservation system, I think; the glomerular kidney is perfectly suitable for living in fresh water, but the business of living immersed, inside and out, for a creature with a salty inside means that the osmotic pressure inside is going to be higher than outside, so that the kidneys are going to have to be pumping virtually all the time. Under the circumstances we'd best step up production of urine, and that means the antidiuretic function of the pituitary gland is going to have to be abrogated, for all practical purposes."

"What about respiration?"

"Hm," Saltonstall said. "I suppose book-lungs, like some of the arachnids have. They can be supplied by intercostal spiracles. They're gradually adaptable to atmosphere-breathing, if our colonist ever decides to come out of the water. Just to provide for that possibility, I'd suggest that the nose be retained, maintaining the nasal cavity as a part of the otological system, but cutting off the cavity from the larynx with a membrane of cells that are supplied with oxygen by direct irrigation, rather than by the circulatory system. Such a membrane wouldn't survive for many generations, once the creature took to living out of the water even for part of its lifetime; it'd go through two or three generations as an amphibian, and then one day it'd suddenly find itself breathing through its larynx again."

"Ingenious," Chatvieux said.

"Also, Dr. Chatvieux, I'd suggest that we have it adopt sporulation. As an aquatic animal, our colonist is going to have an indefinite life-span, but we'll have to give it a breeding cycle of about six weeks to keep up its numbers during the learning period; so there'll have to be a definite break of some duration in its active year. Otherwise it'll hit the population problem before it's learned enough to cope with it."

"And it'd be better if our colonists could winter over inside a good, hard shell," Eunice Wagner added in agreement. "So sporulation's the obvious answer. Many other microscopic creatures have it."

"Microscopic?" Phil said incredulously.

"Certainly," Chatvieux said, amused. "We can't very well crowd a six-foot man into a two-foot puddle. But that raises a question. We'll have tough competition from the rotifers, and some of them aren't strictly microscopic; for that matter even some of the protozoa can be seen with the naked eye, just barely, with dark-field illumination. I don't think your average colonist should run much under 250 microns, Saltonstall. Give them a chance to slug it out."

"I was thinking of making them twice that big."

"Then they'd be the biggest animals in their environment," Eunice Wagner pointed out, "and won't ever develop any skills. Besides, if you make them about rotifer size, it will give them an incentive for pushing out the castle-building rotifers, and occupying the castles themselves, as dwellings."

Chatvieux nodded. "All right, let's get started. While the pantropes are being calibrated, the rest of us can put our heads together on leaving a record for these people. We'll micro-engrave the record on a set of corrosion-proof metal leaves, of a size our colonists can handle conveniently. We can tell them, very simply, what happened, and plant a few suggestions that there's more to the universe than what they find in their puddles. Some day they may puzzle it out."

"Question," Eunice Wagner said. "Are we going to tell them they're microscopic? I'm opposed to it. It may saddle their entire early history with a gods-and-demons mythology that they'd be better off without."

"Yes, we are," Chatvieux said; and la Ventura could tell by the change in the tone of his voice that he was speaking now as their senior on the expedition. "These people will be of the race of men, Eunice. We want them to win their way back into the community of men. They are not toys, to be protected from the truth forever in a fresh-water womb."

"Besides," Saltonstall observed, "they won't get the record translated at any time in their early history. They'll have to develop a written language of their own, and it will be impossible for us to leave them any sort of Rosetta Stone or other key. By the time they can decipher the truth, they should be ready for it."

"I'll make that official," Venezuelos said unexpectedly. And that was that.

And then, essentially, it was all over. They contributed the cells that the pantropes would need. Privately, la Ventura and Joan Heath went to Chatvieux and asked to contribute jointly; but the scientist said that the microscopic men were to be haploid, in order to give them a minute cellular structure, with nuclei as small as Earthly rickettsiae, and therefore each person had to give germ-cells individually—there would be no use for zygotes. So even that consolation was denied them; in death they would have no children, but be instead as alone as ever.

They helped, as far as they could, with the text of the message which was to go on the metal leaves. They had their personality patterns recorded. They went through the motions. Already they were beginning to be hungry; the sea-crayfish, the only things on Hydrot big enough to eat, lived in water too deep and cold for subsistence fishing.

After la Ventura had set his control board to rights—a useless gesture, but a habit he had been taught to respect, and which in an obscure way made things a little easier to bear—he was out of it. He sat by himself at the far end of the rock ledge, watching Tau Ceti go redly down, chucking pebbles into the nearest pond.

After a while Joan Heath came silently up behind him, and sat down too. He took her hand. The glare of the red sun was almost extinguished now, and together they watched it go, with la Ventura, at least, wondering somberly which nameless puddle was to be his Lethe.

He never found out, of course. None of them did.

Cycle One

In a forgotten corner of the galaxy, the watery world of Hydrot hurtles endlessly around the red star, Tau Ceti. For many months its single small continent has been snowbound, and the many pools and lakes which dot the continent have been locked in the grip of the ice. Now, however, the red sun swings closer and closer to the zenith in Hydrot's sky; the snow rushes in torrents toward the eternal ocean, and the ice recedes toward the shores of the lakes and ponds . . .

1

The first thing to reach the consciousness of the sleeping Lavon was a small, intermittent scratching sound. This was followed by a disquieting sensation in his body, as if the world—and Lavon with it—were being rocked back and forth. He stirred uneasily, without opening his eyes. His vastly slowed metabolism made him feel inert and queasy, and the rocking did not help. At his slight motion, however, both the sound and the motion became more insistent.

It seemed to take days for the fog over his brain to clear, but whatever was causing the disturbance would not let him rest. With a groan he forced his eyelids open and made an abrupt gesture with one webbed hand. By the waves of phosphorescence which echoed away from his fingers at the motion, he could see that the smooth amber walls of his spherical shell were unbroken. He tried to peer through them, but he could see nothing but darkness outside. Well, that was natural; the amnionic fluid inside the spore would generate light, but ordinary water did not, no matter how vigorously it was stirred.

Whatever was outside the sphere was rocking it again, with the same whispering friction against its shell. Probably some nosey diatom, Lavon thought sleepily, trying to butt its way through an object it was too stupid to go around. Or some early hunter, yearning for a taste of the morsel inside the spore. Well, let it worry itself; Lavon had no intention of breaking the shell just yet. The fluid in which he had slept for so many months had held his body processes static, and had slowed his mind. Once out into the water, he would have to start breathing and looking for food again, and he could tell by the unrelieved darkness outside that it was too early in the spring to begin thinking about that.

He flexed his fingers reflectively, in the disharmonic motion from little finger to thumb that no animal but man can copy, and watched the widening wavefronts of greenish light rebound in larger arcs from the curved spore walls. Here he was, curled up quite comfortably in a little amber ball, where he could stay until even the depths were warm and light. At this moment there was probably still some ice on the sky, and certainly there would not be much to eat as yet. Not that there was ever much, what with the voracious rotifers coming awake too with the first gust of warm water—

The rotifers! That was it. There was a plan afoot to drive them out. Memory returned in an unwelcome rush. As if to help it, the spore rocked again. That was probably one of the Protos, trying to awaken him; nothing man-eating ever came to the Bottom this early. He had left an early call with the Paras, and now the time had come, as cold and early and dark as he had thought he wanted it.

Reluctantly, Lavon uncurled, planting his webbed toes and arching his backbone as hard as he could, pressing with his whole body against his amber prison. With small, sharp, crepitating sounds, a network of cracks raced through the translucent shell.

Then the spore wall dissolved into a thousand brittle shards, and he was shivering violently with the onslaught of the icy water. The warmer fluid of his winter cell dissipated silently, a faint glowing fog. In the brief light he saw, not far from him, a familiar shape: a transparent, bubble-filled cylinder, a colorless slipper of jelly, spirally grooved, almost as long as he was tall. Its surface was furred with gently vibrating fine hairs, thickened at the base.

The light went out. The Proto said nothing; it waited while Lavon choked and coughed, expelling the last remnants of the spore fluid from his book-lungs and sucking in the pure, ice-cold water.

"Para?" Lavon said at last. "Already?"

"Already," the invisible cilia vibrated in even, emotionless tones. Each separate hair-like process buzzed at an independent, changing rate; the resulting sound waves spread through the water, intermodulating, reinforcing or cancelling each other. The aggregate wave-front, by the time it reached human ears, was rather eerie, but nevertheless recognizable human speech. "This is the time, Lavon."

"Time and more than time," another voice said from the returned darkness. "If we are to drive Flosc from his castles."

"Who's that?" Lavon said, turning futilely toward the new voice.

"I am Para also, Lavon. We are sixteen since the awakening. If you could reproduce as rapidly as we—"

"Brains are better than numbers," Lavon said. "As the Eaters will find out soon enough."

"What shall we do, Lavon?"

The man drew up his knees and sank to the cold mud of the Bottom to think. Something wriggled under his buttocks and a tiny spirillum corkscrewed away, identifiable only by feel. He let it go; he was not hungry yet, and he had the Eaters—the rotifers—to think about. Before long they would be swarming in the upper reaches of the sky, devouring everything, even men when they could catch them, even their natural enemies the Protos now and then. And whether or not the Protos could be organized to battle them was a question still to be tested.

Brains are better than numbers; even that, as a proposition, was still to be tested. The Protos, after all, were intelligent after their fashion; and they knew their world, as the men did not. Lavon could still remember how hard it had been for him to get straight in his head the various clans of beings in this world, and to make sense of their confused names; his tutor Shar had drilled him unmercifully until it had begun to penetrate.

When you said "Man," you meant creatures that, generally speaking, looked alike. The bacteria were of three kinds, the rods and the globes and the spirals, but they were all tiny and edible, so he had learned to differentiate them quickly. When it came to the Protos, identification became a real problem. Para here was a Proto, but he certainly looked very different from Stent and his family, and the family of Didin was unlike both. Anything, as it turned out, that was not green and had a visible nucleus was a Proto, no matter how strange its shape might be. The Eaters were all different, too, and some of them were as beautiful as the fruiting crowns of waterplants; but all of them were deadly, and all had the whirling crown of cilia which could suck you into the incessantly grinding mastax in a moment. Everything which was green and had an engraved shell of glass, Shar had called a diatom, dredging the strange word as he dredged them all from some Bottom in his skull which none of the rest of them could reach, and even Shar could not explain.

Lavon arose quickly. "We need Shar," he said. "Where is his spore?"

"On a plant frond, far up near the sky."

Idiot! The old man would never think of safety. To sleep near the sky, where he might be snatched up and borne off by any Eater to chance by when he emerged, sluggish with winter's long sleep! How could a wise man be so foolish?

"We'll have to hurry. Show me the way."

"Soon; wait," one of the Paras said. "You cannot see. Noc is foraging nearby." There was a small stir in the texture of the darkness as the swift cylinder shot away.

"Why do we need Shar?" the other Para said.

"For his brains, Para. He is a thinker."

"But his thoughts are water. Since he taught the Protos man's language, he has forgotten to think of the Eaters. He thinks forever of the mystery of how man came here. It is a mystery—even the Eaters are not like man. But understanding it will not help us to live."

Lavon turned blindly toward the creature. "Para, tell me something. Why do the Protos side with us? With man, I mean? Why do you need us? The Eaters fear you."

There was a short silence. When the Para spoke again, the vibrations of its voice were more blurred than before, more even, more devoid of any understandable feeling.

"We live in this world," the Para said. "We are of it. We rule it. We came to that state long before the coming of men, in long warfare with the Eaters. But we think as the Eaters do, we do not plan, we share our knowledge and we exist. Men plan; men lead; men are different from each other; men want to remake the world. And they hate the Eaters, as we do. We will help."

"And give up your rule?"

"And give it up, if the rule of men is better. That is reason. Now we can go; Noc is coming back with light."

Lavon looked up. Sure enough, there was a brief flash of cold light far overhead, and then another. In a moment the spherical Proto had dropped into view, its body flaring regularly with blue-green pulses. Beside it darted the second Para.

"Noc brings news," the second Para said. "Para is twenty-four. The Syn are awake by thousands along the sky. Noc spoke to a Syn colony, but they will not help us; they all expect to be dead before the Eaters awake."

"Of course," said the first Para. "That always happens. And the Syn are plants; why should they help the Protos?"

"Ask Noc if he'll guide us to Shar," Lavon said impatiently.

The Noc gestured with its single short, thick tentacle. One of the Paras said, "That is what he is here for."

"Then let's go. We've waited long enough."

The mixed quartet soared away from the Bottom through the liquid darkness.

"No," Lavon snapped. "Not a second longer. The Syn are awake, and Notholca of the Eaters is due right after that. You know that as well as I do, Shar. Wake up!"

"Yes, yes," the old man said fretfully. He stretched and yawned. "You're always in such a hurry, Lavon. Where's Phil? He made his spore near mine." He pointed to a still-unbroken amber sphere sealed to a leaf of the water-plant one tier below. "Better push him off; he'll be safer on the Bottom."

"He would never reach the Bottom," Para said. "The thermocline has formed."

Shar looked surprised. "It has? Is it as late as all that? Wait while I get my records together." He began to search along the leaf in the debris and the piled shards of his spore. Lavon looked impatiently about, found a splinter of stonewort, and threw it heavy end first at the bubble of Phil's cell just below. The spore shattered promptly, and the husky young man tumbled out, blue with shock as the cold water hit him.

"Wough!" he said. "Take it easy, Lavon." He looked up. "The old man's awake? Good. He insisted on staying up here for the winter, so of course I had to stay too."

"Aha," Shar said, and lifted a thick metal plate about the length of his forearm and half as wide. "Here is one of them. Now if only I haven't misplaced the other—"

Phil kicked away a mass of bacteria. "Here it is. Better give them both to a Para, so they won't burden you. Where do we go from here, Lavon? It's dangerous up this high. I'm just glad a Dicran hasn't already shown up."

"I here," something droned just above them.

Instantly, without looking up, Lavon flung himself out and down into the open water, turning his head to look back over his shoulder only when he was already diving as fast as he could go. Shar and Phil had evidently sprung at the same instant. On the next frond above where Shar had spent his winter was the armored, trumpet-shaped body of the rotifer Dicran, contracted to leap after them.

The two Protos came curving back out of nowhere. At the same moment, the bent, shortened body of Dicran flexed in its armor plate, straightened, came plunging toward them. There was a soft *plop* and Lavon found himself struggling in a fine net, as tangled and impassible as the matte of a lichen. A second such sound was followed by a muttered imprecation from Phil. Lavon struck out fiercely, but he was barely able to wriggle in the web of wiry, transparent stuff.

"Be still," a voice which he recognized as Para's throbbed

100

behind him. He managed to screw his head around, and then kicked himself mentally for not having realized at once what had happened. The Paras had exploded the trichocysts which lay like tiny cartridges beneath their pellicles; each one cast forth a liquid which solidified upon contact with the water in a long slender thread. It was their standard method of defense.

Farther down, Shar and Phil drifted with the second Para in the heart of a white haze, like creatures far gone in mold. Dicran swerved to avoid it, but she was evidently unable to give up; she twisted and darted around them, her corona buzzing harshly, her few scraps of the human language forgotten. Seen from this distance, the rotation of the corona was revealed as an illusion, created by the rhythm of pulsation of the individual cilia, but as far as Lavon was concerned the point was solely technical and the distance was far too short. Through the transparent armor Lavon could also see the great jaws of Dicran's mastax, grinding away mechanically at the fragments which poured into her unheeding mouth.

High above them all, Noc circled indecisively, illuminating the whole group with quick, nervous flashes of his blue light. He was a flagellate, and had no natural weapons against the rotifer; why he was hanging around drawing attention to himself Lavon could not imagine.

Then, suddenly, he saw the reason: a barrel-like creature about Noc's size, ringed with two rows of cilia and bearing a ram-like prow. "Didin!" he shouted, unnecessarily. "This way!"

The Proto swung gracefully toward them and seemed to survey them, though it was hard to tell how he could see them without eyes. The Dicran saw him at the same time and began to back slowly away, her buzzing rising to a raw snarl. She regained the plant and crouched down.

For an instant Lavon thought she was going to give up, but experience should have told him that she lacked the sense. Suddenly the lithe, crouched body was in full spring again, this time straight at Didin. Lavon yelled an incoherent warning.

The Proto didn't need it. The slowly cruising barrel darted to one side and then forward, with astonishing speed. If he could sink that poisoned seizing-organ into a weak point in the rotifer's armor—

Noc mounted higher to keep out of the way of the two fighters, and in the resulting weakened light Lavon could not see what was happening, though the furious churning of the water and the buzzing of the Dicran continued.

After a while the sounds seemed to be retreating; Lavon crouched in the gloom inside the Para's net, listening intently. Finally there was silence.

"What's happened?" he whispered tensely.

"Didin does not say."

More eternities went by. Then the darkness began to wane as Noc dropped cautiously toward them.

"Noc, where did they go?"

Noc signaled with his tentacle and turned on his axis toward Para. "He says he lost sight of them. Wait—I hear Didin."

Lavon could hear nothing; what the Para "heard" was some one of the semi-telepathic impulses which made up the Proto's own language.

"He says Dicran is dead."

"Good! Ask him to bring the body back here."

There was a short silence. "He says he will bring it. What good is a dead rotifer, Lavon?"

"You'll see," Lavon said. He watched anxiously until Didin glided backwards into the lighted area, his poisonous ram sunk deep into the flaccid body of the rotifer, which, after the delicately-organized fashion of its kind, was already beginning to disintegrate.

"Let me out of this net, Para."

The Proto jerked sharply for a fraction of a turn on its long axis, snapping the threads off at the base; the movement had to be made with great precision, or its pellicle would tear as well. The tangled mass rose gently with the current and drifted off over the abyss.

Lavon swam forward and, seizing one buckled edge of Dicran's armor, tore away a huge strip of it. His hands plunged into the now almost shapeless body and came out again holding two dark spheroids: eggs.

"Destroy these, Didin," he ordered. The Proto obligingly slashed them open.

"Hereafter," Lavon said, "that's to be standard procedure with every Eater you kill."

"Not the males," one of the Para pointed out.

"Para, you have no sense of humor. All right, not the males —but nobody kills the males anyhow, they're harmless." He looked down grimly at the inert mass. "Remember—destroy the eggs. Killing the beasts isn't enough. We want to wipe out the whole race."

"We never forget," Para said emotionlessly.

The band of over two hundred humans, with Lavon and Shar and a Para at its head, fled swiftly through the warm, light waters of the upper level. Each man gripped a wood splinter, or a fragment of lime chipped from stonewort, as a club; and two hundred pairs of eyes darted watchfully from side to side. Cruising over them was a squadron of twenty Didins, and the rotifers they encountered only glared at them from single red eyespots, making no move to attack. Overhead, near the sky, the sunlight was filtered through a thick layer of living creatures, fighting and feeding and spawning, so that all the depths below were colored a rich green. Most of this heavily populated layer was made up of algae and diatoms, and there the Eaters fed unhindered. Sometimes a dying diatom dropped slowly past the army.

The spring was well advanced; the two hundred, Lavon thought, probably represented all of the humans who had survived the winter. At least no more could be found. The others—nobody would ever know how many—had awakened too late in the season, or had made their spores in exposed places, and the rotifers had snatched them up. Of the group, more than a third were women. That meant that in another forty days, if they were unmolested, they could double the size of their army.

If they were unmolested. Lavon grinned and pushed an agitated colony of Eudorina out of his way. The phrase reminded him of a speculation Shar had brought forth last year: If Para were left unmolested, the oldster had said, he could reproduce fast enough to fill this whole universe with a solid mass of Paras before the season was out. Nobody, of course, ever went unmolested in this world; nevertheless, Lavon meant to cut the odds for people considerably below anything that had heretofore been thought of as natural.

His hand flashed up, and down again. The darting squadrons plunged after him. The light on the sky faded rapidly, and after a while Lavon began to feel slightly chilly. He signaled again. Like dancers, the two hundred swung their bodies in mid-flight, plunging now feet first toward the Bottom. To strike the thermocline in this position would make their passage through it faster, getting them out of the upper level where every minute, despite the convoy of Protos, concentrated danger.

Lavon's feet struck a yielding surface, and with a splash he was over his head in icy water. He bobbed up again, feeling the icy division drawn across his shoulders. Other splashes began to sound all along the thermocline as the army struck it, although, since there was water above and below, Lavon could not see the actual impacts.

Now they would have to wait until their body temperatures fell. At this dividing line of the universe, the warm water ended and the temperature dropped rapidly, so that the water below was much denser and buoyed them up. The lower level of cold reached clear down to the Bottom—an area which the rotifers, who were not very clever, seldom managed to enter.

A moribund diatom drifted down beside Lavon, the greenish-yellow of its body fading to a sick orange, its beautifully-marked, oblong, pillbox-like shell swarming with greedy bacteria. It came to rest on the thermocline, and the transparent caterpillar tread of jelly which ran around it moved feebly, trying vainly to get traction on the sliding water interface. Lavon reached out a webbed hand and brushed away a clot of vibrating rods which had nearly forced its way into the shell through a costal opening.

"Thank . . ." the diatom said, in an indistinct, whispering voice. And again, "Thank . . . Die . . ." The gurgling whisper faded. The caterpillar tread shifted again, then was motionless.

"It is right," a Para said. "Why do you bother with those creatures? They are stupid. Nothing can be done for them."

Lavon did not try to explain. He felt himself sinking slowly, and the water about his trunk and legs no longer seemed cold, only gratefully cool after the stifling heat of that he was breathing. In a moment the cool still depths had closed over his head. He hovered until he was reasonably sure that all the rest of his army was safely through, and the long ordeal of search for survivors in the upper level really ended. Then he twisted and streaked for the Bottom, Phil and Para beside him, Shar puffing along with the vanguard.

A stone loomed; Lavon surveyed it in the half-light. Almost immediately he saw what he had hoped to see: the sand-built house of a caddis-worm, clinging to the mountainous slopes of the rock. He waved in his special cadre and pointed.

Cautiously the men spread out in a U around the stone, the mouth of the U facing the same way as the opening of the worm's masonry tube. A Noc came after them, drifting like a star-shell above the peak; one of the Paras approached the door of the worm's house, buzzing defiantly. Under cover of this challenge the men at the back of the U settled on the rock and began to creep forward. The house was three times as tall as they were; the slimy black sand grains of which it was composed were as big as their heads.

There was a stir inside, and after a moment the ugly head of the worm peered out, weaving uncertainly at the buzzing Para which had disturbed it. The Para drew back, and the worm, in a kind of blind hunger, followed it. A sudden lunge brought it nearly halfway out of its tube.

Lavon shouted. Instantly the worm was surrounded by a howling horde of two-legged demons, who beat and prodded it mercilessly with fists and clubs. Somehow it made a sound, a kind of bleat as unlikely as the bird-like whistle of a fish, and began to slide backwards into its home—but the rear guard had already broken in back there. It jerked forward again, lashing from side to side under the flogging.

There was only one way now for the great larva to go, and the demons around it kept it going that way. It fell toward the Bottom down the side of the rock, naked and ungainly, shaking its blind head and bleating.

Lavon sent five Didin after it. They could not kill it, for it was far too huge to die under their poison, but they could sting it hard enough to keep it travelling. Otherwise, it would be almost sure to return to the rock to start a new house.

Lavon settled on an abutment and surveyed his prize with satisfaction. It was more than big enough to hold his entire clan—a great tubular hall, easily defended once the breach in the rear wall was rebuilt, and well out of the usual haunts of the Eaters. The muck the caddis-worm had left behind would have to be cleaned up, guards posted, vents knocked out to keep the oxygen-poor water of the depths in motion inside. It was too bad that the amoebae could not be detailed to scavenge the place, but Lavon knew better than to issue such an order. The Fathers of the Protos could not be asked to do useful work; that had been made very clear.

He looked around at his army. They were standing around him in awed silence, looking at the spoils of their attack upon the largest creature in the world. He did not think they would ever again feel as timid toward the Eaters. He stood up quickly.

"What are you gaping at?" he shouted. "It's yours, all of it. Get to work!"

Old Shar sat comfortably upon a pebble which had been hollowed out and cushioned with spirogyra straw. Lavon stood nearby at the door, looking out at the maneuvers of his legions. They numbered more than three hundred now, thanks to the month of comparative quiet which they had enjoyed in the great hall, and they handled their numbers well in the aquatic drill which Lavon had invented for them. They swooped and turned above the rock, breaking and reassembling their formations, fighting a sham battle with invisible opponents whose shape they could remember only too well.

"Noc says there's all kinds of quarreling going on among the Eaters," Shar said. "They didn't believe we'd joined with the Protos at first, and then they didn't believe we'd all worked together to capture the hall. And the mass raid we had last week scared them. They'd never tried anything of the kind before, and they *knew* it wouldn't fail. Now they're fighting with each other over why it did. Cooperation is something new to this world, Lavon; it's making history."

"History?" Lavon said, following his drilling squadrons with a technical eye. "What's that?"

"These." The old man leaned over one arm of the pebble and touched the metal plates which were always with him. Lavon turned to follow the gesture, incuriously. He knew the plates well enough—the pure uncorroded shining, graven deeply on both sides with characters no-one, not even Shar, could read. The Protos called the plates *Not-stuff*—neither wood nor flesh nor stone.

"What good is that? I can't read it. Neither can you."

"I've got a start, Lavon. I know the plates are written in our language. Look at the first word: *ha ii ss tuh oh or ee* —exactly the right number of characters for 'history'. That can't be a coincidence. And the next two words have to be 'of the'. And going on from there, using just the characters I already know—" Shar bent and traced in the sand with a stick a new train of characters: *i/terste//ar e//e/ition.*

"What's that?"

"It's a start, Lavon. Just a start. Some day we'll have more."

Lavon shrugged. "Perhaps, when we're safer. We can't afford to worry about that kind of thing now. We've never had that kind of time, not since the First Awakening."

The old man frowned down at the characters in the sand. "The First Awakening. Why does everything seem to stop there? I can remember in the smallest detail nearly everything that happened to me since then. But what happened to our childhoods, Lavon? None of us who survived the First Awakening seems to have had one. Who were our parents?

Why were we so ignorant of the world, and yet grown men and women, all of us?"

"And the answer is in the plates?"

"I hope so," Shar said. "I believe it is. But I don't know. The plates were beside me in the spore at the First Awakening. That's all I know about them, except that there's nothing else like them in the world. The rest is deduction, and I haven't gotten very far with it. Some day . . . some day."

"I hope so too," Lavon said soberly. "I don't mean to mock, Shar, or to be impatient. I've got questions, too; we all have. But we're going to have to put them off for a while. Suppose we never find the whole answer?"

"Then our children will."

"But there's the heart of the problem, Shar: we have to live to have children. And make the kind of a world in which they'll have time to study. Otherwise—"

Lavon broke off as a figure darted between the guards at the door of the hall and twisted to a halt.

"What news, Phil?"

"The same," Phil said, shrugging with his whole body. His feet touched the floor. "The Flosc's castles are going up all along the bar; they'll be finished with them soon, and then we won't dare to get near them. Do you still think you can drive them out?"

Lavon nodded.

"But why?"

"First, for effect. We've been on the defensive so far, even though we've made a good job of it. We'll have to follow that up with an attack of our own if we're going to keep the Eaters confused. Second, the castles Flosc builds are all tunnels and exits and entrances—much better than wormhouses for us. I hate to think of what would have happened if the Eaters had thought of blockading us inside this hall. And we need an outpost in enemy country, Phil, where there are Eaters to kill."

"This is enemy country," Phil said. "Stephanost is a Bottom-dweller."

"But she's only a trapper, not a hunter. Any time we want to kill her, we can find her right where we left her last. It's the leapers like Dicran and Notholca, the swimmers like Rotar, the colony-builders like Flosc that we have to wipe out first."

"Then we'd better start now, Lavon. Once the castles are finished—"

"Yes. Get your squads together, Phil. Shar, come on; we're leaving the hall."

"To raid the castles?"

"Of course."

Shar picked up his plates.

"You'd better leave those here; they'll be in your way in the fighting."

"No," Shar said determinedly. "I don't want them out of my sight. They go along."

3

Vague forebodings, all the more disturbing because he had felt nothing quite like them ever before, passed like clouds of fine silt through Lavon's mind as the army swept away from the hall on the Bottom and climbed toward the thermocline. As far as he could see, everything seemed to be going as he had planned it. As the army moved, its numbers were swelled by Protos who darted into its ranks from all sides. Discipline was good; and every man was armed with a long, seasoned splinter, and from each belt swung a stonewort-flake hand-axe, held by a thong run through a hole Shar had taught them all how to drill. There would probably be much death before the light of today faded, but death was common enough on any day, and this time it should heavily disfavor the Eaters.

But there was a chill upon the depths that Lavon did not like, and a suggestion of a current in the water which was unnatural below the thermocline. A great many days had been consumed in collecting the army, recruiting from stragglers, and in securing the hall. The intensive breeding which had followed, and the training of the new-born and the newly recruited, had taken still more time, all of it essential, but all irrevocable. If the chill and the current marked the beginning of the fall turnover . . .

If it did, nothing could be done about it. The turnover could no more be postponed than the coming of day or night. He signaled to the nearest Para.

The glistening torpedo veered toward him. Lavon pointed up.

"Here comes the thermocline, Para. Are we pointed right?"

"Yes, Lavon. That way is the place where the Bottom rises toward the sky. Flosc's castles are on the other side, where she will not see us."

"The sand bar that runs out from the north. Right. It's getting warmer. Here we go."

108

Lavon felt his flight suddenly quicken, as if he had been shot like a seed from some invisible thumb and forefinger. He looked over his shoulder to watch the passage of the rest through the temperature barrier, and what he saw thrilled him as sharply as any awakening. Up to now he had had no clear picture of the size of his forces, or the three-dimensional beauty of their dynamic, mobile organization. Even the Protos had fitted themselves into the squads; pattern after pattern of power came soaring after Lavon from the Bottom: first a single Noc bowling along like a beacon to guide all the rest, then an advance cone of Didin to watch for individual Eaters who might flee to give the alarm, and then the men, and the Protos, who made up the main force, in tight formations as beautiful as the elementary geometry from which Shar had helped derive them.

The sand-bar loomed ahead, as vast as any mountain range. Lavon soared sharply upward, and the tumbled, raw-boned boulders of the sand grains swept by rapidly beneath him in a broad, stony flood. Far beyond the ridge, towering up to the sky through glowing green obscurity, were the befronded stems of the plant jungle which was their objective. It was too dim with distance to allow him to see the clinging castles of the Flosc yet, but he knew that the longest part of the march was over. He narrowed his eyes and cleft the sunlit waters with driving, rapid strokes of his webbed hands and feet. The invaders poured after him over the crest of the bar in an orderly torrent.

Lavon swung his arm in a circle. Silently, the following squadrons glided into a great paraboloid, its axis pointed at the jungle. The castles were visible now; until the formation of the army, they had been the only products of close co-operation that this world had ever seen. They were built of single brown tubes, narrow at the base, attached to each other in a random pattern in an ensemble as delicate as a branching coral. In the mouth of each tube was a rotifer, a Flosc, distinguished from other Eaters by the four-leaf-clover of its corona, and by the single, prehensile finger springing from the small of its back, with which it ceaselessly molded its brown spittle into hard pellets and cemented them carefully to the rim of its tube.

As usual, the castles chilled Lavon's muscles with doubt. They were perfect, and they had always been one of the major, stony flowers of summer, long before there had been any First Awakening, or any men. And there was surely something wrong with the water in the upper level; it was warm and sleepy. The heads of the Flosc hummed content-

edly at the mouths of their tubes; everything was as it should
be, as it had always been; the army was a fantasm, the attack
a failure before it had begun—

Then they were spied.

The Flosc vanished instantly, contracting violently into
their tubes. The placid humming of their continuous feeding
upon everything that passed was snuffed out; spared motes
drifted about the castle in the light.

Lavon found himself smiling. Not long ago, the Flosc would
only have waited until the humans were close enough, and
then would have sucked them down, without more than a
few struggles here and there, a few pauses in the humming
while the out-size morsels were enfolded and fed into the
grinders. Now, instead, they hid; they were afraid.

"Go!" he shouted at the top of his voice. "Kill them! Kill
them while they're down!"

The army behind him swept after him with a stunning
composite shout.

Tactics vanished. A petalled corona unfolded in Lavon's
face, and a buzzing whirlpool spun him toward its black
heart. He slashed wildly with his edged wooden splinter.

The sharp edge sliced deeply into the ciliated lobes. The
rotifer screamed like a siren and contracted into her tube,
closing her wounded face. Grimly, Lavon followed.

It was pitch dark inside the castle, and the raging currents
of pain which flowed past him threw him from one pebbly
wall to another. He gritted his teeth and probed with the
splinter. It bit into a yielding surface at once, and another
scream made his ears ring, mixed with mangled bits of words
in Lavon's own language, senseless and horrible with agony.
He slashed at them until they stopped, and continued to slash
until he could control his terror.

As soon as he was able, he groped in the torn corpse for
the eggs. The point found their life and pricked it. Trembling,
he pulled himself back to the mouth of the tube, and without
stopping to think pushed himself off at the first Eater to
pass it.

The thing was a Dicran; she doubled viciously upon him
at once. Even the Eaters had learned something about co-
operation. And the Dicrans fought well in open water. They
were the best possible reinforcements the Flosc could have
called.

The Dicran's armor turned the point of Lavon's splinter
easily. He jabbed frantically, hoping to hit a joint, but the
agile creature gave him no time to aim. She charged him

110

irresistibly, and her humming corona folded down around his head, pinned his forearms to his sides—

The Eater heaved convulsively and went limp. Lavon half slashed, half tore his way free. A Didin was drawing back, pulling out its seizing-organ. The body floated downward.

"Thanks," Lavon gasped. The Proto darted off without replying; it lacked sufficient cilia to imitate human speech. Possibly it lacked the desire as well; the Didins were not sociable.

A tearing whirlpool sprang into being again around him, and he flexed his sword-arm. In the next five dreamlike minutes he developed a technique for dealing with the sessile, sucking Flosc. Instead of fighting the current and swinging the splinter back and forth against it, he gave in to the vortex, rode with it, and braced the splinter between his feet, point down. The results were even better than he had hoped. The point, driven by the full force of the Flosc's own trap, pierced the soft, wormlike body half through while it gaped for the human quarry. After each encounter, Lavon doggedly went through the messy ritual of destroying the eggs.

At last he emerged from a tube to find that the battle had drifted away from him. He paused on the edge to get his breath back, clinging to the rounded, translucent bricks and watching the fighting. It was difficult to make any military sense out of the melee, but as far as he could tell the rotifers were getting the worst of it. They did not know how to meet so carefully organized an attack, and they were not in any real sense intelligent.

The Didin were ranging from one side of the fray to the other, in two tight, vicious efficient groups, englobing and destroying free-swimming rotifers in whole flocks at a time. Lavon saw no fewer than half a dozen Eaters trapped by teams of Paras, each pair dragging a struggling victim in a trichocyst net remorselessly toward the Bottom, where she would inevitably suffocate. He was astonished to see one of the few Nocs that had accompanied his army scouring a cringing Rotar with its virtually harmless tentacle; the Eater seemed too astonished to fight back, and Lavon for once knew just how she felt.

A figure swam slowly and tiredly up to him from below. It was old Shar, puffing hard. Lavon reached a hand down to him and hauled him onto the lip of the tube. The man's face wore a frightening expression, half shock, half pure grief.

"Gone, Lavon," he said. "Gone. Lost."

"What? What's gone? What's the matter?"

"The plate. You were right. I should have known." He sobbed convulsively.

"What plate? Calm down. What happened? Did you lose one of the history plates—or both of them?"

Slowly his tutor seemed to be recovering control of his breathing. "One of them," he said wretchedly. "I dropped it in the fight. I hid the other one in an empty Flosc tube. But I dropped the first one—the one I'd just begun to decipher. It went all the way down to the Bottom, and I couldn't get free to go after it—all I could do was watch it go, spinning down into the darkness. We could sift the mud forever and never find it."

He dropped his face into his hands. Perched on the edge of the brown tube in the green glow of the waters, he looked both pathetic and absurd. Lavon did not know what to say; even he realized that the loss was major and perhaps final, that the awesome blank in their memories prior to the First Awakening might now never be filled. How Shar felt about it he could comprehend only dimly.

Another human figure darted and twisted toward him. "Lavon!" Phil's voice cried. "It's working, it's working! The swimmers are running away, what's left of them. There are still some Flosc in the castles, hiding in the darkness. If we could only lure them out in the open—"

Jarred back to the present, Lavon's mind raced over the possibilities. The whole attack could still fail if the Flosc entrenched themselves successfully. After all, a big kill had not been the only object; they had started out to capture the castles.

"Shar—do these tubes connect with each other?"

"Yes," the old man said without interest. "It's a continuous system."

Lavon sprang out upon the open water. "Come on, Phil. We'll attack them from the rear." Turning, he plunged into the mouth of the tube, Phil on his heels.

It was very dark, and the water was fetid with the odor of the tube's late owner, but after a moment's groping Lavon found the opening which lead into the next tube. It was easy to tell which way was out because of the pitch of the walls; everything the Flosc built had a conical bore, differing from the next tube only in size. Determinedly Lavon worked his way toward the main stem, going always down and in.

Once they passed beneath an opening beyond which the water was in furious motion, and out of which poured muffled sounds of shouting and a defiant buzz. Lavon stopped to probe through the hole with his sword. The rotifer gave a shrill, startled shriek and jerked her wounded tail upward, involuntarily releasing her toe-hold upon the walls of the tube. Lavon moved on, grinning. The men above would do the rest.

Reaching the central stem at last, Lavon and Phil went methodically from one branch to another, spearing the surprised Eaters from behind or cutting them loose so that the men outside could get at them as they drifted upward, propelled by the drag of their own coronas. The trumpet shape of the tubes prevented the Eaters from turning to fight, and from following them through the castle to surprise them from behind; each Flosc had only the one room, which she never left.

The gutting of the castles took hardly fifteen minutes. The day was just beginning to end when Lavon emerged with Phil at the mouth of a turret to look down upon the first City of Man.

He lay in darkness, his forehead pressed against his knees, as motionless as a dead man. The water was stuffy, cold, the blackness complete. Around him were the walls of a tube of Flosc's castle; above him a Para laid another sand grain upon a new domed roof. The rest of the army rested in other tubes, covered with other new stony caps, but there was no sound of movement or of voices. It was as quiet as a necropolis.

Lavon's thoughts were slow and bitter as drugged syrup. He had been right about the passage of the seasons. He had had barely enough time to bring all his people from the hall to the castles before the annual debacle of the fall overturn. Then the waters of the universe had revolved once, bringing the skies to the Bottom, and the Bottom to the skies, and then mixing both. The thermocline was destroyed until next year's spring overturn would reform it.

And inevitably, the abrupt change in temperature and oxygen concentration had started the spore-building glands again. The spherical amber shell was going up around Lavon now, and there was nothing he could do about it. It was an involuntary process, as dissociated from his control as the beating of his heart. Soon the light-generating oil which filled the spore would come pouring out, expelling and replacing the cold, foul water, and then sleep would come . . .

And all this had happened just as they had made a real gain, had established themselves in enemy country, had come within reach of the chance to destroy the Eaters wholesale and forever. Now the eggs of the Eaters had been laid, and next year it would have to be done all over again. And there was the loss of the plate; he had hardly begun to reflect upon what that would mean for the future.

There was a soft *chunk* as the last sand grain fell into place on the roof. The sound did not quite bring the final wave of despair against which he had been fighting in advance. Instead, it seemed to carry with it a wave of obscure contentment, with which his consciousness began to sink more and more rapidly toward sleep. They were safe, after all. They could not be ousted from the castle. And there would be fewer Eaters next year, because of all the eggs that had been destroyed, and the layers of those eggs . . . There was one plate still left . . .

Quiet and cold; darkness and silence.

In a forgotten corner of the galaxy, the watery world of Hydrot hurtles endlessly around the red star, Tau Ceti. For many months life has swarmed in its lakes and pools, but now the sun retreats from the zenith, and the snow falls, and the ice advances from the eternal ocean. Life sinks once more toward slumber, simulating death, and the battles and lusts and ambitions and defeats of a thousand million microscopic creatures retreat in to the limbo where such things matter not at all.

No, such things matter not at all when winter reigns on Hydrot; but winter is an inconstant king.

Cycle Two

1

Old Shar set down the thick, ragged-edged metal plate at last, and gazed instead out the window of the castle, apparently resting his eyes on the glowing green-gold obscurity of the summer waters. In the soft fluorescence which played down upon him, from the Noc dozing impassively in the groined vault of the chamber, Lavon could see that he was in fact a young man. His face was so delicately formed as to suggest that it had not been many seasons since he had first emerged from his spore.

But of course there had been no real reason to have expected an old man. All the Shars had been referred to traditionally as "old" Shar. The reason, like the reasons for everything else, had been forgotten, but the custom had persisted. The adjective at least gave weight and dignity to the office—

that of the center of wisdom of all the people, as each Lavon had been the center of authority.

The present Shar belonged to the generation XVI, and hence would have to be at least two seasons younger than Lavon himself. If he was old, it was only in knowledge.

"Lavon, I'm going to have to be honest with you," Shar said at last, still looking out of the tall, irregular window. "You've come to me at your maturity for the secrets on the metal plate, just as your predecessors did to mine. I can give some of them to you—but for the most part, I don't know what they mean."

"After so many generations?" Lavon asked, surprised. "Wasn't it Shar III who made the first complete translation? That was a long time ago."

The young man turned and looked at Lavon with eyes made dark and wide by the depths into which they had been staring. "I can read what's on the plate, but most of it seems to make no sense. Worst of all, the record's incomplete. You didn't know that? It is. One of the plates was lost in a battle during the first war with the Eaters, while these castles were still in their hands."

"What am I here for, then?" Lavon said. "Isn't there anything of value on the remaining plate? Did they really contain 'the wisdom of the Creators,' or is that another myth?"

"No. No, it's true," Shar said slowly, "as far as it goes."

He paused, and both men turned and gazed at the ghostly creature which had appeared suddenly outside the window. Then Shar said gravely, "Come in, Para."

The slipper-shaped organism, nearly transparent except for the thousands of black-and-silver granules and frothy bubbles which packed its interior, glided into the chamber and hovered, with a muted whirring of cilia. For a moment it remained silent, speaking telepathically to the Noc floating in the vault, after the ceremonious fashion of all the Protos. No human had ever intercepted one of these colloquies, but there was no doubt about their reality; humans had used them for long-range communication for generations.

Then the Para's cilia vibrated once more. "We are arrived, Shar and Lavon, according to the custom."

"And welcome," said Shar. "Lavon, let's leave this matter of the plates for a while, until you hear what Para has to say; that's a part of the knowledge Lavons must have as they come into their office, and it comes before the plates. I can give you some hints of what we are. First Para has to tell you something about what we aren't."

Lavon nodded, willingly enough, and watched the Proto as

it settled gently to the surface of the hewn table at which Shar had been sitting. There was in the entity such a perfection and economy of organization, such a grace and surety of movement, that he could hardly believe in his own new-won maturity. Para, like all the Protos, made him feel, not perhaps poorly thought-out, but at least unfinished.

"We know that in this universe there is logically no place for man," the gleaming, now immobile cylinder upon the table droned abruptly. "Our memory is the common property of all our races. It reaches back to a time when there were no such creatures as man here, nor any even remotely like men. It remembers also that once upon a day there were men here, suddenly, and in some numbers. Their spores littered the Bottom; we found the spores only a short time after our season's Awakening, and inside them we saw the forms of men, slumbering.

"Then men shattered their spores and emerged. At first they seemed helpless, and the Eaters devoured them by scores, as in those days they devoured everything that moved. But that soon ended. Men were intelligent, active. And they were gifted with a trait, a character, possessed by no other creature in this world. Not even the savage Eaters had it. Men organized us to exterminate the Eaters, and therein lay the difference. Men had initiative. We have the word now, which you gave us, and we apply it, but we still do not know what the thing is that it labels."

"You fought beside us," Lavon said.

"Gladly. We would never have thought of that war by ourselves, but it was good and brought good. Yet we wondered. We saw that men were poor swimmers, poor walkers, poor crawlers, poor climbers. We saw that men were formed to make and use tools, a concept we still do not understand, for so wonderful a gift is largely wasted in this universe, and there is no other. What good are tool-useful members such as the hands of men? We do not know. It seems plain that so radical a thing should lead to a much greater rulership over the world than has, in fact, proven to be possible for men."

Lavon's head was spinning. "Para, I had no notion that you people were philosophers."

"The Protos are old," Shar said. He had again turned to look out the window, his hands locked behind his back. "They aren't philosphers, Lavon, but they are remorseless logicians. Listen to Para."

"To this reasoning there could be but one outcome," the Para said. "Our strange ally, Man, was like nothing else in this universe. He was and is unfitted for it. He does not belong

116

here; he has been——adapted. This drives us to think that there are other universes besides this one, but where these universes might lie, and what their properties might be, it is impossible to imagine. We have no imagination, as men know."

Was the creature being ironic? Lavon could not tell. He said slowly. "Other universes? How could that be true?"

"We do not know," the Para's uninflected voice hummed. Lavon waited, but obviously the Proto had nothing more to say.

Shar had resumed sitting on the window sill, clasping his knees, watching the come and go of dim shapes in the lighted gulf. "It is quite true," he said. "What is written on the plate makes it plain. Let me tell you now what it says.

"We were made, Lavon. We were made by men who were not as we are, but men who were our ancestors all the same. They were caught in some disaster, and they made us, and put us here in our universe—so that, even though they had to die, the race of men would live."

Lavon surged up from the woven spirogyra mat upon which he had been sitting. "You must think I'm a fool," he said sharply.

"No. You're our Lavon; you have a right to know the facts. Make what you like of them." Shar swung his webbed toes back into the chamber. "What I've told you may be hard to believe, but it seems to be so; what Para says backs it up. Our unfitness to live here is self-evident. I'll give you some examples:

"The past four Shars discovered that we won't get any farther in our studies until we learn how to control heat. We've produced enough heat chemically to show that even the water around us changes when the temperature gets high enough—or low enough, that we knew from the beginning. But there we're stopped."

"Why?"

"Because heat produced in open water is carried off as rapidly as it's produced. Once we tried to enclose that heat, and we blew up a whole tube of the castle and killed everything in range; the shock was terrible. We measured the pressures that were involved in that explosion, and we discovered that no substance we know could have resisted them. Theory suggests some stronger substances—but *we need heat to form them!*

"Take our chemistry. We live in water. Everything seems to dissolve in water, to some extent. How do we confine a chemical test to the crucible we put it in? How do we maintain a solution at one dilution? I don't know. Every avenue

117

leads me to the same stone door. We're thinking creatures, Lavon, but there's something drastically wrong in the way we think about this universe we live in. It just doesn't seem to lead to results."

Lavon pushed back his floating hair futilely. "Maybe you're thinking about the wrong results. We've had no trouble with warfare, or crops, or practical things like that. If we can't create much heat, well, most of us won't miss it; we don't need more than we have. What's the other universe supposed to be like, the one our ancestors lived in? Is it any better than this one?"

"I don't know," Shar admitted. "It was so different that it's hard to compare the two. The metal plate tells a story about men who were travelling from one place to another in a container that moved by itself. The only analogue I can think of is the shallops of diatom shells that our youngsters used to sled along the thermocline; but evidently what's meant is something much bigger.

"I picture a huge shallop, closed on all sides, big enough to hold many people—maybe twenty or thirty. It had to travel for generations through some kind of medium where there wasn't any water to breathe, so the people had to carry their own water and renew it constantly. There were no seasons; no ice formed on the sky, because there couldn't be any sky in a closed shallop; and so there was no spore formation.

"Then the shallop was wrecked somehow. The people in it knew they were going to die. They made us, and put us here, as if we were their children. Because they had to die, they wrote their story on the plates, to tell us what had happened. I suppose we'd understand it better if we had the plate Shar I lost during the war—but we don't."

"The whole thing sounds like a parable," Lavon said, shrugging. "Or a song. I can see why you don't understand it. What I can't see is why you bother to try."

"Because of the plate," Shar said. "You've handled it yourself now, so you know that we've nothing like it. We have crude, impure metals we've hammered out, metals that last for a while and then decay. But the plate shines on, generation after generation. It doesn't change; our hammers and our graving tools break against it; the little heat we can generate leaves it unharmed. That plate wasn't formed in our universe—and that one fact makes every word on it important to me. Someone went to a great deal of trouble to make those plates indestructible, and to give them to us. Someone to whom the word 'stars' was important enough to be worth fourteen repetitions, despite the fact that the word doesn't seem to mean anything. I'm ready to think that if our makers repeated a word even twice on a record that seems likely to last forever, then it's important for us to know what it means."

Layon stood up once more.

"All these extra universes and huge shallops and meaningless words—I can't say that they don't exist, but I don't see what difference it makes," he said. "The Shars of a few generations ago spent their whole lives breeding better algae crops for us, and showing us how to cultivate them, instead of living haphazardly on bacteria. Farther back, the Shars devised war engines, and war plans. All that was work worth doing. The Lavons of those days evidently got along without the metal plate and its puzzles, and saw to it that the Shars did, too. Well, as far as I'm concerned, you're welcome to the plate, if you like it better than crop improvement—but I think it ought to be thrown away."

"All right," Shar said, shrugging. "If you don't want it, that ends the traditional interview. We'll go our—"

There was a rising drone from the table-top. The Para was lifting itself, waves of motion passing over its cilia, like the waves which went silently across the fruiting stalks of the fields of delicate fungi with which the Bottom was planted. It had been so silent that Lavon had forgotten it; he could tell from Shar's startlement that Shar had, too.

"This is a great decision," the waves of sound washing from the creature throbbed. "Every Proto has heard it, and agrees with it. We have been afraid of this metal plate for a long time, afraid that men would learn to understand it and follow what it says to some secret place, leaving the Protos behind. Now we are not afraid."

"There wasn't anything to be afraid of," Lavon said indulgently.

"No Lavon before you, Lavon, had ever said so," the Para said. "We are glad. We will throw the plate away, as Lavon orders."

With that, the shining creature swooped toward the embrasure. With it, it bore away the remaining plate, which had been resting under it on the tabletop, suspended delicately in the curved tips of its supple ventral cilia. Inside its pellucid body, vacuoles swelled to increase its buoyancy and enable it to carry the heavy weight.

With a cry, Shar plunged through the water toward the window.

"Stop, Para!"

But Para was already gone, so swiftly that it had not even heard the call. Shar twisted his body and brought up one shoulder against the tower wall. He said nothing. His face was enough. Lavon could not look into it for more than an instant.

The shadows of the two men began to move slowly along the uneven cobbled floor. The Noc descended toward them from the vault, its tentacle stirring the water, its internal light flaring and fading irregularly. It, too, drifted through the window after its cousin, and sank slowly away toward the Bottom. Gently its living glow dimmed, flickered in the depths, and winked out.

2

For many days, Lavon was able to avoid thinking much about the loss. There was always a great deal of work to be done. Maintenance of the castles was a never-ending task. The thousand dichotomously-branching wings tended to crumble with time, especially at their bases where they sprouted from one another, and no Shar had yet come forward with a mortar as good as the rotifer-spittle which had once held them together. In addition, the breaking through of windows and the construction of chambers in the early days had been haphazard and often unsound. The instinctive architecture of the Eaters, after all, had not been meant to meet the needs of human occupants.

And then there were the crops. Men no longer fed precariously upon passing bacteria snatched to the mouth; now there were the drifting mats of specific water-fungi and algae, and the mycelia on the Bottom, rich and nourishing, which had been bred by five generations of Shars. These had to be tended constantly to keep the strains pure, and to keep the older and less intelligent species of the Protos from grazing on them. In this latter task, to be sure, the more intricate and far-seeing Proto types cooperated, but men were needed to supervise.

There had been a time, after the war with the Eaters, when it had been customary to prey upon the slow-moving and stupid diatoms, whose exquisite and fragile glass shells were so easily burst, and who were unable to learn that a friendly voice did not necessarily mean a friend. There were still people who would crack open a diatom when no one else was looking, but they were regarded as barbarians, to the puzzlement of the Protos. The blurred and simple-minded speech of the gorgeously engraved plants had brought them into the category of community pets—a concept which the Protos were utterly unable to grasp, especially since men admitted that diatoms on the half-frustrule were delicious.

Lavon had had to agree, very early, that the distinction was tiny. After all, humans did eat the desmids, which differed from the diatoms only in three particulars: Their shells were flexible, they could not move (and for that matter neither could all but a few groups of diatoms), and they did not speak. Yet to Lavon, as to most men, there did seem to be some kind of distinction, whether the Protos could see it or not, and that was that. Under the circumstances he felt that it was a part of his duty, as the hereditary leader of men, to protect the diatoms from the occasional poachers who browsed upon them, in defiance of custom, in the high levels of the sunlit sky.

Yet Lavon found it impossible to keep himself busy enough to forget that moment when the last clues to Man's origin and destination had been seized, on authority of his own careless exaggeration, and borne away into dim space.

It might be possible to ask Para for the return of the plate, explain that a mistake had been made. The Protos were creatures of implacable logic, but they respected men, were used to illogic in men, and might reverse their decision if pressed—

We are sorry. The plate was carried over the bar and released in the gulf. We will have the Bottom there searched, but . . .

With a sick feeling he could not repress, Lavon knew that that would be the answer, or something very like it. When the Protos decided something was worthless, they did not hide it in some chamber like old women. They threw it away —efficiently.

Yet despite the tormenting of his conscience, Lavon was nearly convinced that the plate was well lost. What had it ever done for Man, except to provide Shars with useless things to think about in the late seasons of their lives? What the Shars themselves had done to benefit Man, here, in the water, in the world, in the universe, had been done by direct experimentation. No bit of useful knowledge had ever come from the plates. There had never been anything in the second plate, at least, but things best left unthought. The Protos were right.

Lavon shifted his position on the plant frond, where he had been sitting in order to overlook the harvesting of an experimental crop of blue-green, oil-rich algae drifting in a clotted mass close to the top of the sky, and scratched his back gently against the coarse bole. The Protos were seldom wrong, after all. Their lack of creativity, their inability to think an original thought, was a gift as well as a limitation. It allowed them to see and feel things at all times as they were—not as they hoped they might be, for they had no ability to hope, either.

"La-von! Laa-vah-on!"

The long halloo came floating up from the sleepy depths. Propping one hand against the top of the frond, Lavon bent and looked down. One of the harvesters was looking up at him, holding loosely the adze with which he had been splitting free from the raft the glutinous tetrads of the algae.

"I'm up here. What's the matter?"

"We have the ripened quadrant cut free. Shall we tow it away?"

"Tow it away," Lavon said, with a lazy gesture. He leaned back again. At the same instant, a brilliant reddish glory burst into being above him, and cast itself down toward the depths like mesh after mesh of the finest-drawn gold. The great light which lived above the sky during the day, brightening or dimming according to some pattern no Shar ever had fathomed, was blooming again.

Few men, caught in the warm glow of that light, could resist looking up at it—especially when the top of the sky itself wrinkled and smiled just a moment's climb or swim away. Yet, as always, Lavon's bemused upward look gave him back nothing but his own distorted, bobbling reflection, and a reflection of the plant on which he rested.

Here was the upper limit, the third of the three surfaces of the universe. The first surface was the Bottom, where the water ended.

The second surface was the thermocline, definite enough in summer to provide good sledding, but easily penetrable if you knew how.

The third surface was the sky. One could no more pass through that surface than one could penetrate the Bottom, nor was there any better reason to try. There the universe ended. The light which played over it daily, waxing and waning as it chose, seemed to be one of its properties.

Toward the end of the season, the water gradually became colder and more difficult to breathe, while at the same time the light grew duller and stayed for shorter periods between darknesses. Slow currents started to move. The high waters turned chill and started to fall. The Bottom mud stirred and

122

smoked away, carrying with it the spores of the fields of fungi. The thermocline tossed, became choppy, and melted away. The sky began to fog with particles of soft silt carried up from the Bottom, the walls, the corners of the universe. Before very long, the whole world was cold, inhospitable, flocculent with yellowing, dying creatures. The world died until the first tentative current of warm water broke the winter silence.

That was how it was when the second surface vanished. If the sky were to melt away . . .

"Lavon!"

Just after the long call, a shining bubble rose past Lavon. He reached out and poked it, but it bounded away from his sharp thumb. The gas bubbles which rose from the Bottom in late summer were almost invulnerable—and when some especially hard blow or edge did penetrate them, they broke into smaller bubbles which nothing could touch, leaving behind a remarkably bad smell.

Gas. There was no water inside a bubble. A man who got inside a bubble would have nothing to breathe.

But, of course, it was impossible to enter a bubble. The surface tension was too strong. As strong as Shar's metal plate. As strong as the top of the sky.

As strong as the top of the sky. And above that—once the bubble was broken—a world of gas instead of water? Were all worlds bubbles of water drifting in gas?

If it were so, travel between them would be out of the question, since it would be impossible to pierce the sky to begin with. Nor did the infant cosmography include any provisions for Bottoms for the worlds.

And yet some of the local creatures did burrow *into* the Bottom, quite deeply, seeking something in those depths which was beyond the reach of Man. Even the surface of the ooze, in high summer, crawled with tiny creatures for which mud was a natural medium. And though many of the entities with which man lived could not pass freely between the two countries of water which were divided by the thermocline, men could and did.

And if the new universe of which Shar had spoken existed at all, it had to exist beyond the sky, where the light was. Why could not the sky be passed, after all? The fact that bubbles could sometimes be broken showed that the surface skin had formed between water and gas wasn't completely invulnerable. Had it ever been tried?

Lavon did not suppose that one man could butt his way through the top of the sky, any more than he could burrow

123

into the Bottom, but there might be ways around the difficulty. Here at his back, for instance, was a plant which gave every appearance of continuing beyond the sky; its upper fronds broke off and were bent back only by a trick of reflection.

It had always been assumed that the plants died where they touched the sky. For the most part, they did, for frequently the dead extension could be seen, leached and yellow, the boxes of its component cells empty, floating imbedded in the perfect mirror. But some were simply chopped off, like the one which sheltered him now. Perhaps that was only an illusion, and instead it soared indefinitely into some other place—some place where men might once have been born, and might still live . . .

Both plates were gone. There was only one other way to find out.

Determinedly, Lavon began to climb toward the wavering mirror of the sky. His thorn-thumbed feet trampled obliviously upon the clustered sheaths of fragile stippled diatoms. The tulip-heads of Vortae, placid and murmurous cousins of Para, retracted startledly out of his way upon coiling stalks, to make silly gossip behind him.

Lavon did not hear them. He continued to climb doggedly toward the light, his fingers and toes gripping the plant-bole.

"Lavon! Where are you going? Lavon!"

He leaned out and looked down. The man with the adze, a doll-like figure, was beckoning to him from a patch of blue-green retreating over a violet abyss. Dizzily he looked away, clinging to the bole; he had never been so high before. He had, of course, nothing to fear from falling, but the fear was in his heritage. Then he began to climb again.

After a while, he touched the sky with one hand. He stopped to breathe. Curious bacteria gathered about the base of his thumb where blood from a small cut was fogging away, scattered at his gesture, and wriggled mindlessly back toward the dull red lure.

He waited until he no longer felt winded, and resumed climbing. The sky pressed down against the top of his head, against the back of his neck, against his shoulders. It seemed to give slightly, with a tough, frictionless elasticity. The water here was intensely bright, and quite colorless. He climbed another step, driving his shoulders against that enormous weight.

It was fruitless. He might as well have tried to penetrate a cliff.

Again he had to rest. While he panted, he made a curious

discovery. All around the bole of the water plant, the steel surface of the sky curved upward, making a kind of sheath. He found that he could insert his hand into it—there was almost enough space to admit his head as well. Clinging closely to the bole, he looked up into the inside of the sheath, probing it with his injured hand. The glare was blinding.

There was a kind of soundless explosion. His whole wrist was suddenly encircled in an intense, impersonal grip, as if it were being cut in two. In blind astonishment, he lunged upward.

The ring of pain travelled smoothly down his upflung arm as he rose, was suddenly around his shoulders and chest. Another lunge and his knees were being squeezed in the circular vise. Another—

Something was horribly wrong. He clung to the bole and tried to gasp, but there was—nothing to breathe.

The water came streaming out of his body, from his mouth, his nostrils, the spiracles in his sides, spurting in tangible jets. An intense and fiery itching crawled over the surface of his body. At each spasm, long knives ran into him, and from a great distance he heard more water being expelled from his book-lungs in an obscene, frothy sputtering. Inside his head, a patch of fire began to eat away at the floor of his nasal cavity.

Lavon was drowning.

With a final convulsion, he kicked himself away from the splintery bole, and fell. A hard impact shook him; and then the water, who had clung to him so tightly when he had first attempted to leave her, took him back with cold violence.

Sprawling and tumbling grotesquely, he drifted, down and down and down, toward the Bottom.

3

For many days, Lavon lay curled insensibly in his spore, as if in the winter sleep. The shock of cold which he had felt on re-entering his native universe had been taken by his body as a sign of coming winter, as it had taken the ozygen-starvation of his brief sojourn above the sky. The spore-forming glands had at once begun to function.

Had it not been for this, Lavon would surely have died. The danger of drowning disappeared even as he fell, as the air bubbled out of his lungs and readmitted the life-giving water. But for acute desiccation and third degree sunburn, the sunken universe knew no remedy. The healing amnionic fluid generated by the spore-forming glands, after the transparent amber sphere had enclosed him, offered Lavon his only chance.

The brown sphere, quiescent in the eternal winter of the Bottom, was spotted after some days by a prowling ameba. Down there the temperature was always an even 4°, no matter what the season, but it was unheard of that a spore should be found there while the high epilimnion was still warm and rich in oxygen.

Within an hour, the spore was surrounded by scores of astonished protos, jostling each other to bump their blunt eyeless prows against the shell. Another hour later, a squad of worried men came plunging from the castles far above to press their own noses against the transparent wall. Then swift orders were given.

Four Para grouped themselves about the amber sphere, and there was a subdued explosion as their trichocysts burst. The four Paras thrummed and lifted, tugging.

Lavon's spore swayed gently in the mud and then rose slowly, entangled in the fine web. Nearby, a Noc cast a cold pulsating glow over the operation, for the benefit of the baffled knot of men. The sleeping figure of Lavon, head bowed, knees drawn up into its chest, revolved with an absurd solemnity inside the shell as it was moved.

"Take him to Shar, Para."

The young Shar justified, by minding his own business, the traditional wisdom with which his hereditary office had invested him. He observed at once that there was nothing he could do for the encysted Lavon which would not be classifiable as simple meddling.

He had the sphere deposited in a high tower room of his castle, where there was plenty of light and the water was warm, which should suggest to the estivating form that spring was again on the way. Beyond that, he simply sat and watched, and kept his speculations to himself.

Inside the spore, Lavon's body seemed to be rapidly shedding its skin, in long strips and patches. Gradually, his curious shrunkenness disappeared. His withered arms and legs and sunken abdomen filled out again.

The days went by while Shar watched. Finally he could discern no more changes, and, on a hunch, had the spore taken up to the topmost battlements of the tower, into the direct daylight.

An hour later, Lavon moved in his amber prison.

126

He uncurled and stretched, turned blank eyes up toward the light. His expression was that of a man who had not yet awakened from a ferocious nightmare. His whole body shone with a strange pink newness.

Shar knocked gently on the walls of the spore. Lavon turned his blind face toward the sound, life coming into his eyes. He smiled tentatively and braced his hands and feet against the inner wall of the shell.

The whole sphere fell abruptly to pieces with a sharp crackling. The amnionic fluid dissipated around him and Shar, carrying away with it the suggestive odor of a bitter struggle against death.

Lavon stood among the shards and looked at Shar silently. At last he said:

"Shar—I've been above the sky."

"I know," Shar said gently.

Again Lavon was silent. Shar said, "Don't be humble, Lavon. You've done an epoch-making thing. It nearly cost you your life. You must tell me the rest—all of it."

"The rest?"

"You taught me a lot while you slept. Or are you still opposed to 'useless' knowledge?"

Lavon could say nothing. He no longer could tell what he knew from what he wanted to know. He had only one question left, but he could not utter it. He could only look dumbly into Shar's delicate face.

"You have answered me," Shar said, even more gently than before. "Come, my friend; join me at my table. We will plan our journey to the stars."

There were five of them around Shar's big table: Shar himself, Lavon, and the three assistants assigned by custom to the Shars from the families Than, Tanol and Stravol. The duties of these three men—or, sometimes, women—under many previous Shars had been simple and onerous: to put into effect in the field the genetic changes in the food crops which the Shar himself had worked out in little, in laboratory tanks and flats. Under other Shars more interested in metalworking or in chemistry, they had been smudged men—diggers, rock-splitters, fashioners and cleaners of apparatus.

Under Shar XVI, however, the three assistants had been more envied than usual among the rest of Lavon's people, for they seemed to do very little work of any kind. They spent long hours of every day talking with Shar in his chambers, poring over records, making miniscule scratch-marks on slate, or just looking intently at simple things about which there was no obvious mystery. Sometimes they actually worked with Shar in his laboratory, but mostly they just sat.

Shar XVI had, as a matter of fact, discovered certain rudimentary rules of inquiry which, as he explained it to Lavon, he had recognized as tools of enormous power. He had become more interested in passing these on to future workers than in the seductions of any specific experiment, the journey to the stars perhaps excepted. The Than, Tanol and Stravol of his generation were having scientific method pounded into their heads, a procedure they maintained was sometimes more painful than heaving a thousand rocks.

That they were the first of Lavon's people to be taxed with the problem of constructing a spaceship was, therefore, inevitable. The results lay on the table: three models, made of diatom-glass, strands of algae, flexible bits of cellulose, flakes of stonewort, slivers of wood, and organic glues collected from the secretions of a score of different plants and animals.

Lavon picked up the nearest one, a fragile spherical construction inside which little beads of dark-brown lava—actually bricks of rotifer-spittle painfully chipped free from the wall of an unused castle—moved freely back and forth in a kind of ball-bearing race. "Now whose is this one?" he said, turning the sphere curiously to and fro.

"That's mine," Tanol said. "Frankly, I don't think it comes anywhere near meeting all the requirements. It's just the only design I could arrive at that I think we could build with the materials and knowledge we have to hand now."

"But how does it work?"

"Hand it here a moment, Lavon. This bladder you see inside at the center, with the hollow spirogyra straws leading out from it to the skin of the ship, is a buoyancy tank. The idea is that we trap ourselves a big gas-bubble as it rises from the Bottom and install it in the tank. Probably we'll have to do that piecemeal. Then the ship rises to the sky on the buoyancy of the bubble. The little paddles, here along these two bands on the outside, rotate when the crew—that's these bricks you hear shaking around inside—walks a treadmill that runs around the inside of the hull; they paddle us over to the edge of the sky. I stole that trick from the way Didin gets about. Then we pull the paddles in—they fold over into slots, like this—and, still by weight-transfer from the inside, we roll ourselves up the slope until we're out in space. When we hit another world and enter the water again, we let the gas out of the tank gradually through the exhaust tubes represented by these straws, and sink down to a landing at a controlled rate."

"Very ingenious," Shar said thoughtfully. "But I can foresee some difficulties. For one thing, the design lacks stability."

"Yes, it does," Tanol agreed. "And keeping it in motion is going to require a lot of footwork. But if we were to sling a freely-moving weight from the center of gravity of the machine, we could stabilize it at least partly. And the biggest expenditure of energy involved in the whole trip is going to be getting the machine up to the sky in the first place, and with this design that's taken care of—as a matter of fact, once the bubble's installed, we'll have to keep the ship tied down until we're ready to take off."

"How about letting the gas out?" Lavon said. "Will it go out through those little tubes when we want it to? Won't it just cling to the walls of the tubes instead? The skin between water and gas is pretty difficult to deform—to that I can testify."

Tanol frowned. "That I don't know. Don't forget that the tubes will be large in the real ship, not just straws as they are in the model."

"Bigger than a man's body?" Than said.

"No, hardly. Maybe as big through as a man's head, at the most."

"Won't work," Than said tersely. "I tried it. You can't lead a bubble through a pipe that small. As Lavon says, it clings to the inside of the tube and won't be budged unless you put pressure behind it—lots of pressure. If we build this ship, we'll just have to abandon it once we hit our new world; we won't be able to set it down anywhere."

"That's out of the question," Lavon said at once. "Putting aside for the moment the waste involved, we may have to use the ship again in a hurry. Who knows what the new world will be like? We're going to have to be able to leave it again if it turns out to be impossible to live in."

"Which is your model, Than?" Shar said.

"This one. With this design, we do the trip the hard way —crawl along the Bottom until it meets the sky, crawl until we hit the next world, and crawl wherever we're going when we get there. No aquabatics. She's treadmill-powered, like Tanol's, but not necessarily man-powered; I've been thinking a bit about using motile diatoms. She steers by varying the power on one side or the other. For fine steering we can also hitch a pair of thongs to opposite ends of the rear axle and swivel her that way."

Shar looked closely at the tube-shaped model and pushed it experimentally along the table a little way. "I like that," he said presently. "It sits still when you want it to. With Than's spherical ship, we'd be at the mercy of any stray current at home or in the new world—and for all I know there may be currents of some sort in space, too, gas currents perhaps. Lavon, what do you think?"

"How would we build it?" Lavon said. "It's round in cross-section. That's all very well for a model, but how do you make a really big tube of that shape that won't fall in on itself?"

"Look inside, through the front window," Than said. "You'll see beams that cross at the center, at right angles to the long axis. They hold the walls braced."

"That consumes a lot of space," Stravol objected. By far the quietest and most introspective of the three assistants, he had not spoken until now since the beginning of the conference. "You've got to have free passage back and forth inside the ship. How are we going to keep everything operating if we have to be crawling around beams all the time?"

"All right, come up with something better," Than said, shrugging.

"That's easy. We bend hoops."

"Hoops!" Tanol said. "On *that* scale? You'd have to soak your wood in mud for a year before it would be flexible enough, and then it wouldn't have the strength you'd need."

"No, you wouldn't," Stravol said. "I didn't build a ship model, I just made drawings, and my ship isn't as good as Than's by a long distance. But my design for the ship is also tubular, so I did build a model of a hoop-bending machine—that's it on the table. You lock one end of your beam down in a heavy vise, like so, leaving the butt striking out on the other side. Then you tie up the other end with a heavy line, around this notch. Then you run your line around a windlass, and five or six men wind up the windlass, like so. That pulls the free end of the beam down until the notch engages with this key-slot, which you've pre-cut at the other end. Then you un-lock the vise, and there's your hoop; for safety you might drive a peg through the joint to keep the thing from spring-ing open unexpectedly."

"Wouldn't the beam you were using break after it had bent a certain distance?" Lavon asked.

"Stock timber certainly would," Stravol said. "But for this trick you use *green* wood, not seasoned. Otherwise you'd have to soften your beam to uselessness, as Tanol says. But live wood will flex enough to make a good, strong, single-unit hoop—or if it doesn't, Shar, the little rituals with numbers that you've been teaching us don't mean anything after all!"

Shar smiled. "You can easily make a mistake in using num-bers," he said.

"I checked everything."

"I'm sure of it. And I think it's well worth a trial. Anything else to offer?"

"Well," Stravol said, "I've got a kind of live ventilating system I think should be useful. Otherwise, as I said, Than's ship strikes me as the type we should build; my own's hopelessly cumbersome."

"I have to agree," Tanol said regretfully. "But I'd like to try putting together a lighter-than-water ship sometime, maybe just for local travel. If the new world is bigger than ours, it might not be possible to swim everywhere you might want to go."

"That never occurred to me," Lavon exclaimed. "Suppose the new world *is* twice, three times, eight times as big as ours? Shar, is there any reason why that couldn't be?"

"None that I know of. The history plate certainly seems to take all kinds of enormous distances practically for granted. All right, let's make up a composite design from what we have here. Tanol, you're the best draftsman among us, suppose you draw it up. Lavon, what about labor?"

"I've a plan ready," Lavon said. "As I see it, the people who work on the ship are going to have to be on the job full time. Building the vessel isn't going to be an overnight task, or even one that we can finish in a single season, so we can't count on using a rotating force. Besides, this is technical work; once a man learns how to do a particular task, it would be wasteful to send him back to tending fungi just because somebody else has some time on his hands.

"So I've set up a basic force involving the two or three most intelligent hand-workers from each of the various trades. Those people I can withdraw from their regular work without upsetting the way we run our usual concerns, or noticeably increasing the burden on the others in a given trade. They will do the skilled labor, and stick with the ship until it's done. Some of them will make up the crew, too. For heavy, unskilled jobs, we can call on the various seasonal pools of unskilled people without disrupting our ordinary life."

"Good," Shar said. He leaned forward and rested linked hands on the edge of the table—although, because of the webbing between his fingers, he could link no more than the fingertips. "We've really made remarkable progress. I didn't expect that we'd have matters advanced a tenth as far as this by the end of this meeting. But maybe I've overlooked something important. Has anybody any more suggestions, or any questions?"

"I've got a question," Stravol said quietly.

"All right, let's hear it."

"Where are we going?"

There was quite a long silence. Finally Shar said: "Stravol, I can't answer that yet. I could say that we're going to the stars, but since we still have no idea what a star is, that answer wouldn't do you much good. We're going to make this trip because we've found that some of the fantastic things that the history plate says are really so. We know now that the sky can be passed, and that beyond the sky there's a region where there's no water to breathe, the region our ancients called 'space.' Both of these ideas always seemed to be against common sense, but nevertheless we've found that they're true.

"The history plate also says that there are other worlds than ours, and actually that's an easier idea to accept, once you've found out that the other two are so. As for the stars—well, we just don't know yet, we haven't any information at all that would allow us to read the history plate on that subject with new eyes, and there's no point in making wild guesses unless we can test the guesses. The stars are in space, and presumably, once we're out in space, we'll see them and the meaning of the word will become clear. At least we can confidently expect to see some clues—look at all the information we got from Lavon's trip of a few seconds above the sky!

"But in the meantime, there's no point in our speculating in a bubble. We think there are other worlds somewhere, and we're devising means to make the trip. The other questions, the pendant ones, just have to be put aside for now. We'll answer them eventually—there's no doubt in my mind about that. But it may take a long time."

Stravol grinned ruefully. "I expected no more. In a way, I think the whole project in crazy. But I'm in it right out to the end, all the same."

Shar and Lavon grinned back. All of them had the fever, and Lavon suspected that their whole enclosed universe would share it with them before long. He said:

"Then let's not waste a minute. There's still a huge mass of detail to be worked out, and after that, all the hard work will just have begun. Let's get moving!"

The five men arose and looked at each other. Their expressions varied, but in all their eyes there was in addition the same mixture of awe and ambition: the composite face of the shipwright and of the astronaut.

Then they went out, severally, to begin their voyages.

It was two winter sleeps after Lavon's disastrous climb beyond the sky that all work on the spaceship stopped. By then,

Lavon knew that he had hardened and weathered into that temporarily ageless state a man enters after he has just reached his prime; and he knew also that there were wrinkles engraved on his brow, to stay and to deepen.

"Old" Shar, too, had changed, his features losing some of their delicacy as he came into his maturity. Though the wedge-shaped bony structure of his face would give him a withdrawn and poetic look for as long as he lived, participation in the plan had given his expression a kind of executive overlay, which at best made it assume a mask-like rigidity, and at worst coarsened it somehow.

Yet despite the bleeding away of the years, the spaceship was still only a hulk. It lay upon a platform built above the tumbled boulders of the sandbar which stretched out from one wall of the world. It was an immense hull of pegged wood, broken by regularly spaced gaps through which the raw beams of its skeleton could be seen.

Work upon it had progressed fairly rapidly at first, for it was not hard to visualize what kind of vehicle would be needed to crawl through empty space without losing its water; Than and his colleagues had done that job well. It had been recognized, too, that the sheer size of the machine would enforce a long period of construction, perhaps as long as two full seasons; but neither Shar and his assistants nor Lavon had anticipated any serious snag.

For that matter, part of the vehicle's apparent incompleteness was an illusion. About a third of its fittings were to consist of living creatures, which could not be expected to install themselves in the vessel much before the actual takeoff.

Yet time and time again, work on the ship had to be halted for long periods. Several times whole sections needed to be ripped out, as it became more and more evident that hardly a single normal, understandable concept could be applied to the problem of space travel.

The lack of the history plate, which the Para steadfastly refused to deliver up, was a double handicap. Immediately upon its loss, Shar had set himself to reproduce it from memory; but unlike the more religious of his ancestors, he had never regarded it as holy writ, and hence had never set himself to memorizing it word by word. Even before the theft, he had accumulated a set of variant translations of passages presenting specific experimental problems, which were stored in his library, carved in wood. Most of these translations, however, tended to contradict each other, and none of them related to spaceship construction, upon which the original had been vague in any case.

No duplicates of the cryptic characters of the original had ever been made, for the simple reason that there was nothing in the sunken universe capable of destroying the originals, nor of duplicating their apparently changeless permanence. Shar remarked too late that through simple caution they should have made a number of verbatim temporary records —but after generations of green-gold peace, simple caution no longer covers preparation against catastrophe. (Nor, for that matter, does a culture which has to dig each letter of its simple alphabet into pulpy water-logged wood with a flake of stonewort encourage the keeping of records in triplicate.)

As a result, Shar's imperfect memory of the contents of the history plate, plus the constant and millenial doubt as to the accuracy of the various translations, proved finally to be the worst obstacle to progress on the spaceship itself.

"Men must paddle before they can swim," Lavon observed belatedly, and Shar was forced to agree with him.

Obviously, whatever the ancients had known about spaceship construction, very little of that knowledge was usable to a people still trying to build its first spaceship from scratch. In retrospect, it was not surprising that the great hulk rested incomplete upon its platform above the sand boulders, exuding a musty odor of wood steadily losing its strength, two generations after its flat bottom had been laid down.

The fat-faced young man who headed the strike delegation to Shar's chambers was Phil XX, a man two generations younger than Shar, four younger than Lavon. There were crow's-feet at the corners of his eyes, which made him look both like a querulous old man and like an infant spoiled in the spore.

"We're calling a halt to this crazy project," he said bluntly. "We've slaved away our youth on it, but now that we're our own masters, it's over, that's all. It's over."

"Nobody's compelled you," Lavon said angrily.

"Society does; our parents do," a gaunt member of the delegation said. "But now we're going to start living in the real world. Everybody these days knows that there's no other world but this one. You oldsters can hang on to your superstitions if you like. We don't intend to."

Baffled, Lavon looked over at Shar. The scientist smiled and said, "Let them go, Lavon. We have no use for the faint-hearted."

The fat-faced young man flushed. "You can't insult us into going back to work. We're through. Build your own ship to no place!"

"All right," Lavon said evenly. "Go on, beat it. Don't stand

134

around here orating about it. You've made your decisions and we're not interested in your self-justifications. Goodbye."

The fat-faced young man evidently still had quite a bit of heroism to dramatize which Lavon's dismissal had short-circuited. An examination of Lavon's stony face, however, seemed to convince him that he had to take his victory as he found it. He and the delegation trailed ingloriously out the archway.

"Now what?" Lavon asked when they had gone. "I must admit, Shar, that I would have tried to persuade them. We do need the workers, after all."

"Not as much as they need us," Shar said tranquilly. "I know all those young men. I think they'll be astonished at the runty crops their fields will produce next season, after they have to breed them without my advice. Now, how many volunteers have you got for the crew of the ship?"

"Hundreds. Every youngster of the generation after Phil's wants to go along. Phil's wrong about the segment of the populace, at least. The project catches the imagination of the very young."

"Did you give them any encouragement?"

"Sure," Lavon said. "I told them we'd call on them if they were chosen. But you can't take that seriously! We'd do badly to displace our picked group of specialists with youths who have enthusiasm and nothing else."

"That's not what I had in mind, Lavon. Didn't I see a Noc in these chambers somewhere? Oh, there he is, asleep in the dome. Noc!"

The creature stirred its tentacle lazily.

"Noc, I've a message," Shar called. "The Protos are to tell all men that those who wish to go to the next world with the spaceship must come to the staging area right away. Say that we can't promise to take everyone, but that only those who help us to build the ship will be considered at all."

The Noc curled its tentacle again, and appeared to go back to sleep.

4

Lavon turned from the arrangement of speaking-tube megaphones which was his control board and looked at Para. "One last try," he said. "Will you give us back the history plate?"

"No, Lavon. We have never denied you anything before. But this we must."

"You're going with us, though, Para. Unless you give us back the knowledge we need, you'll lose your life if we lose ours."

"What is one Para?" the creature said. "We are all alike. This cell will die; but the Protos need to know how you fare on this journey. We believe you should make it without the plate, for in no other way can we assess the real importance of the plate."

"Then you admit you still have it. What if you can't communicate with your fellows once we're out in space? How do you know that water isn't essential to your telepathy?"

The Proto was silent. Lavon stared at it a moment, then turned deliberately back to the speaking tubes. "Everyone hang on," he said. He felt shaky. "We're about to start. Stravol, is the ship sealed?"

"As far as I can tell, Lavon."

Lavon shifted to another megaphone. He took a deep breath. Already the water seemed stifling, although the ship hadn't moved.

"Ready with one-quarter power. . . . One, two, three, *go*."

The whole ship jerked and settled back into place again. The raphe diatoms along the under hull settled into their niches, their jelly treads turning against broad endless belts of crude caddis-worm leather. Wooden gears creaked, stepping up the slow power of the creatures, transmitting it to the sixteen axles of the ship's wheels.

The ship rocked and began to roll slowly along the sand bar. Lavon looked tensely through the mica port. The world flowed painfully past him. The ship canted and began to climb the slope. Behind him, he could feel the electric silence of Shar, Para, and the two alternate pilots, Than and Stravol, as if their gaze were stabbing directly through his body and on out the port. The world looked different, now that he was leaving it. How had he missed all this beauty before?

The slapping of the endless belts and the squeaking and groaning of the gears and axles grew louder as the slope steepened. The ship continued to climb, lurching. Around it, squadrons of men and Protos dipped and wheeled, escorting it toward the sky.

Gradually the sky lowered and pressed down toward the top of the ship.

"A little more work from your diatoms, Tanol," Lavon said. "Boulder ahead." The ship swung ponderously. "All right, slow them up again. Give us a shove from your side, Tol—no, that's too much—there, that's it. Back to normal; you're still turning us! Tanol, give us one burst to line us up again. Good. All right, steady drive on all sides. It shouldn't be long now."

"How can you think in webs like that?" the Para wondered behind him.

"I just do, that's all. It's the way men think. Overseers, a little more thrust now; the grade's getting steeper."

The gears groaned. The ship nosed up. The sky brightened in Lavon's face. Despite himself, he began to be frightened. His lungs seemed to burn, and in his mind he felt his long fall through nothingness toward the chill slap of the water as if he were experiencing it for the first time. His skin itched and burned. Could he go up there again? Up there into the burning void, the great gasping agony where no life should go?

The sand bar began to level out and the going became a little easier. Up here, the sky was so close that the lumbering motion of the huge ship disturbed it. Shadows of wavelets ran across the sand. Silently, the thick-barreled bands of blue-green algae drank in the light and converted it to oxygen, writhing in their slow mindless dance just under the long mica skylight which ran along the spine of the ship. In the hold, beneath the latticed corridor and cabin floors, whirring Vortae kept the ship's water in motion, fueling themselves upon drifting organic particles.

One by one, the figures wheeling outside about the ship waved arms or cilia and fell back, coasting down the slope of the sand bar toward the familiar world, dwindling and disappearing. There was at last only one single Euglena, half-plant cousin of the Protos, forging along beside the spaceship into the marshes of the shallows. It loved the light, but finally it, too, was driven away into deeper, cooler waters, its single whiplike tentacle undulating placidly as it went. It was not very bright, but Lavon felt deserted when it left.

Where they were going, though, none could follow.

Now the sky was nothing but a thin, resistant skin of water coating the top of the ship. The vessel slowed, and when Lavon called for more power, it began to dig itself in among the sandgrains and boulders.

"That's not going to work," Shar said tensely. "I think we'd better step down the gear-ratio, Lavon, so you can apply stress more slowly."

"All right," Lavon agreed. "Full stop, everybody. Shar, will you supervise gear-changing, please?"

Insane brilliance of empty space looked Lavon full in the face just beyond his big mica bull'seye. It was maddening to be forced to stop here upon the threshold of infinity; and it was dangerous, too. Lavon could feel building in him the old fear of the outside. A few moments more of inaction, he knew with a gathering coldness in his belly, and he would be unable to go through with it.

Surely, he thought, there must be a better way to change gear-ratios than the traditional one, which involved dismantling almost the entire gear-box. Why couldn't a number of gears of different sizes be carried on the same shaft, not necessarily all in action at once, but awaiting use simply by shoving the axle back and forth longitudinally in its sockets? It would still be clumsy, but it could be worked on orders from the bridge and would not involve shutting down the entire machine—and throwing the new pilot into a blue-green funk.

Shar came lunging up through the trap and swam himself to a stop.

"All set," he said. "The big reduction gears aren't taking the strain too well, though."

"Splintering?"

"Yes. I'd go it slow at first."

Lavon nodded mutely. Without allowing himself to stop, even for a moment, to consider the consequences of his words, he called: "Half power."

The ship hunched itself down again and began to move, very slowly indeed, but more smoothly than before. Overhead, the sky thinned to complete transparency. The great light came blasting in. Behind Lavon there was an uneasy stir. The whiteness grew at the front ports.

Again the ship slowed, straining against the blinding barrier. Lavon swallowed and called for more power. The ship groaned like something about to die. It was now almost at a standstill.

"More power," Lavon ground out.

Once more, with infinite slowness, the ship began to move. Gently, it tilted upward.

Then it lunged forward and every board and beam in it began to squall.

"Lavon! Lavon!"

Lavon started sharply at the shout. The voice was coming at him from one of the megaphones, the one marked for the port at the rear of the ship.

"Lavon!"

"What is it? Stop your damn yelling."

"I can see the top of the sky! From the *other* side, from the top side! It's like a big flat sheet of metal. We're going away from it. We're above the sky, Lavon, we're above the sky!"

Another violent start swung Lavon around toward the for-

138

ward port. On the outside of the mica, the water was evaporating with shocking swiftness, taking with it strange distortions and patterns made of rainbows.

Lavon saw space.

It was at first like a deserted and cruelly dry version of the Bottom. There were enormous boulders, great cliffs, tumbled, split, riven, jagged rocks going up and away in all directions, as if scattered at random by some giant.

But it had a sky of its own—a deep blue dome so far away that he could not believe in, let alone estimate, what its distance might be. And in this dome was a ball of reddish-white fire that seared his eyeballs.

The wilderness of rock was still a long way away from the ship, which now seemed to be resting upon a level, glistening plain. Beneath the surface-shine, the plain seemed to be made of sand, nothing but familiar sand, the same substance which had heaped up to form a bar in Lavon's universe, the bar along which the ship had climbed. But the glassy, colorful skin over it—

Suddenly Lavon became conscious of another shout from the megaphone banks. He shook his head savagely and said, "What is it now?"

"Lavon, this is Tol. What have you gotten us into? The belts are locked. The diatoms can't move them. They aren't faking, either; we've rapped them hard enough to make them think we were trying to break their shells, but they still can't give us more power."

"Leave them alone," Lavon snapped. "They can't fake; they haven't enough intelligence. If they say they can't give you more power, they can't."

"Well, then, you get us out of it."

Shar came forward to Lavon's elbow. "We're on a space-water interface, where the surface tension is very high," he said softly. "If you order the wheels pulled up now, I think we'll make better progress for a while on the belly tread."

"Good enough," Lavon said with relief. "Hello below— haul up the wheels."

"For a long while," Shar said, "I couldn't understand the reference of the history plate to 'retractable landing gear,' but it finally occurred to me that the tension along a space-mud interface would hold any large object pretty tightly. That's why I insisted on our building the ship so that we could lift the wheels."

"Evidently the ancients knew their business after all, Shar."

Quite a few minutes later—for shifting power to the belly

139

treads involved another setting of the gear box—the ship was crawling along the shore toward the tumbled rock. Anxiously, Lavon scanned the jagged, threatening wall for a break. There was a sort of rivulet off toward the left which might offer a route, though a dubious one, to the next world. After some thought, Lavon ordered his ship turned toward it.

"Do you suppose that thing in the sky is a 'star'?" he asked. "But there were supposed to be lots of them. Only one is up there—and one's plenty for my taste."

"I don't know," Shar admitted. "But I'm beginning to get a picture of the way the universe is made, I think. Evidently our world is a sort of cup in the Bottom of this huge one. This one has a sky of its own; perhaps it, too, is only a cup in the Bottom of a still huger world, and so on and on without end. It's a hard concept to grasp, I'll admit. Maybe it would be more sensible to assume that all the worlds are cups in this one common surface, and that the great light shines on them all impartially."

"Then what makes it go out every night, and dim even in the day during winter?" Lavon demanded.

"Perhaps it travels in circles, over first one world, then another. How could I know yet?"

"Well, if you're right, it means that all we have to do is crawl along here for a while, until we hit the top of the sky of another world," Lavon said. "Then we dive in. Somehow it seems too simple, after all our preparations."

Shar chuckled, but the sound did not suggest that he had discovered anything funny. "Simple? Have you noticed the temperature yet?"

Lavon had noticed it, just beneath the surface of awareness, but at Shar's remark he realized that he was gradually being stifled. The oxygen content of the water, luckily, had not dropped, but the temperature suggested the shallows in the last and worst part of autumn. It was like trying to breathe soup.

"Than, give us more action from the Vortae," Lavon said. "This is going to be unbearable unless we get more circulation."

There was a reply from Than, but it came to Lavon's ears only as a mumble. It was all he could do now to keep his attention on the business of steering the ship.

The cut or defile in the scattered razor-edged rocks was a little closer, but there still seemed to be many miles of rough desert to cross. After a while, the ship settled into a steady, painfully slow crawling, with less pitching and jerking than before, but also with less progress. Under it, there was now a
140

sliding, grinding sound, rasping against the hull of the ship itself, as if it were treadmilling over some coarse lubricant the particles of which were each as big as a man's head.

Finally Shar said, "Lavon, we'll have to stop again. The sand this far up is dry, and we're wasting energy using the tread."

"Are you sure we can take it?" Lavon asked, gasping for breath. "At least we are moving. If we stop to lower the wheels and change gears again, we'll boil."

"We'll boil if we don't," Shar said calmly. "Some of our algae are dead already and the rest are withering. That's a pretty good sign that we can't take much more. I don't think we'll make it into the shadows, unless we do change over and put on some speed."

There was a gulping sound from one of the mechanics. "We ought to turn back," he said raggedly. "We were never meant to be out here in the first place. We were made for the water, not for this hell."

"We'll stop," Lavon said, "but we're not turning back. That's final."

The words made a brave sound, but the man had upset Lavon more than he dared to admit, even to himself. "Shar," he said, "make it fast, will you?"

The scientist nodded and dived below.

The minutes stretched out. The great red-gold globe in the sky blazed and blazed. It had moved down the sky, far down, so that the light was pouring into the ship directly in Lavon's face, illuminating every floating particle, its rays like long milky streamers. The currents of water passing Lavon's cheek were almost hot.

How could they dare go directly forward into that inferno? The land directly under the "star" must be even hotter than it was here.

"Lavon! Look at Para!"

Lavon forced himself to turn and look at his Proto ally. The great slipper had settled to the deck, where it was lying with only a feeble pulsation of its cilia. Inside, its vacuoles were beginning to swell, to become bloated, pear-shaped bubbles, crowding the granulated cytoplasm, pressing upon the dark nuclei.

"Is . . . is he dying?"

"This cell is dying," Para said, as coldly as always. "But go on—go on. There is much to learn, and you may live, even though we do not. Go on."

"You're—for us now?" Lavon whispered.

"We have alway been for you. Push your folly to the utter-most. We will benefit in the end, and so will Man."

The whisper died away. Lavon called the creature again, but it did not respond.

There was a wooden clashing from below, and then Shar's voice came tinnily from one of the megaphones. "Lavon, go ahead! The diatoms are dying, too, and then we'll be without power. Make it as quickly and directly as you can."

Grimly, Lavon leaned forward. "The 'star' is directly over the land we're approaching."

"It is? It may go lower still and the shadows will get longer. That may be our only hope."

Lavon had not thought of that. He rasped into the banked megaphones. Once more, the ship began to move, a little faster now, but seemingly still at a crawl. The thirty-two wheels rumbled.

It got hotter.

Steadily, with a perceptible motion, the "star" sank in Lavon's face. Suddenly a new terror struck him. Suppose it should continue to go down until it was gone entirely? Blast-ing though it was now, it was the only source of heat. Would not space become bitter cold on the instant—and the ship an expanding, bursting block of ice?

The shadows lengthened menacingly, stretching across the desert toward the forward-rolling vessel. There was no talking in the cabin, just the sound of ragged breathing and the creaking of the machinery.

Then the jagged horizon seemed to rush upon them. Stony teeth cut into the lower rim of the ball of fire, devoured it swiftly. It was gone.

They were in the lee of the cliffs. Lavon ordered the ship turned to parallel the rock-line; it responded heavily, slug-gishly. Far above, the sky deepened steadily, from blue to indigo.

Shar came silently up through the trap and stood beside Lavon, studying that deepening color and the lengthening of the shadows down the beach toward their own world. He said nothing, but Lavon was sure that the same chilling thought was in his mind.

"Lavon."

Lavon jumped. Shar's voice had iron in it. "Yes?"

"We'll have to keep moving. We must make the next world, wherever it is, very shortly."

"How can we dare move when we can't see where we're going? Why not sleep it over—if the cold will let us?"

"It will let us," Shar said. "It can't get dangerously cold up

142

here. If it did, the sky—or what we used to think of as the sky—would have frozen over every night, even in summer. But what I'm thinking about is the water. The plants will go to sleep now. In our world that wouldn't matter; the supply of oxygen there is enough to last through the night. But in this confined space, with so many creatures in it and no supply of fresh water, we will probably smother."

Shar seemed hardly to be involved at all, but spoke rather with the voice of implacable physical laws.

"Furthermore," he said, staring unseeingly out at the raw landscape, "the diatoms are plants, too. In other words, we must stay on the move for as long as we have oxygen and power—and pray that we make it."

"Shar, we had quite a few Protos on board this ship once. And Para there isn't quite dead yet. If he were, the cabin would be intolerable. The ship is nearly sterile of bacteria, because all the protos have been eating them as a matter of course and there's no outside supply of them, either. But still and all there would have been some decay."

Shar bent and tested the pellicle of the motionless Para with a probing finger. "You're right, he's still alive. What does that prove?"

"The Vortae are also alive; I can feel the water circulating. Which proves that it wasn't the heat that hurt Para. *It was the light.* Remember how badly my skin was affected after I climbed beyond the sky? Undiluted starlight is deadly. We should add that to the information from the plate."

"I still don't get the point."

"It's this: We've got three or four Noc down below. They were shielded from the light, and so must be still alive. If we concentrate them in the diatom galleys, the dumb diatoms will think it's still daylight and will go on working. Or we can concentrate them up along the spine of the ship, and keep the algae putting out oxygen. So the question is: Which do we need more, oxygen or power? Or can we split the difference?"

Shar actually grinned. "A brilliant piece of thinking. We may make a Shar out of you some day, Lavon. No, I'd say that we can't split the difference. Noc's light isn't intense enough to keep the plants making oxygen; I tried it once, and the oxygen production was too tiny to matter. Evidently the plants use the light for energy. So we'll have to settle for the diatoms for motive power."

"All right. Set it up that way, Shar."

Lavon brought the vessel away from the rocky lee of the cliff, out onto the smoother sand. All trace of direct light was now gone, although there was still a soft, general glow on the sky.

"Now then," Shar said thoughtfully, "I would guess that there's water over there in the canyon, if we can reach it. I'll go below again and arrange—"

Lavon gasped.

"What's the matter?"

Silently, Lavon pointed, his heart pounding.

The entire dome of indigo above them was spangled with tiny, incredibly brilliant lights. There were hundreds of them, and more and more were becoming visible as the darkness deepened. And far away, over the ultimate edge of the rocks, was a dim red globe, crescented wigh ghostly silver. Near the zenith was another such body, much smaller, and silvered all over . . .

Under the two moons of Hydrot, and under the eternal stars, the two-inch wooden spaceship and its microscopic cargo toiled down the slope toward the drying little rivulet.

5

The ship rested on the Bottom of the canyon for the rest of the night. The great square doors were unsealed and thrown open to admit the raw, irradiated, life-giving water from out-side—and the wriggling bacteria which were fresh food.

No other creatures approached them, either out of curi-osity or for hunting, while they slept, although Lavon had posted guards at the doors just in case. Evidently, even up here on the very floor of space, highly organized creatures were quiescent at night.

But when the first flush of light filtered through the water, trouble threatened.

First of all, there was the bug-eyed monster. The thing was green and had two snapping claws, either one of which could have broken the ship in two like a spirogyra strand. Its eyes were black and globular, on the ends of short columns, and its long feelers were thicker through than a plant bole. It passed in a kicking fury of motion, however, never noticing the ship at all.

"Is that—a sample of the kind of life they have here?" La-von whispered. "Does it all run as big as that?" Nobody an-swered, for the very good reason that nobody knew.

After a while, Lavon risked moving the ship forward against the current, which was slow but heavy. Enormous writing worms whipped past them. One struck the hull a heavy blow, then thrashed on obliviously.

"They don't notice us," Shar said. "We're too small. Lavon, the ancients warned us of the immensity of space, but even when you see it, it's impossible to grasp. And all those stars —can they mean what I think they mean? It's beyond thought, beyond belief!"

"The Bottom's sloping," Lavon said, looking ahead intently. "The walls of the canyon are retreating, and the water's becoming rather silty. Let the stars wait, Shar; we're coming toward the entrance of our new world."

Shar subsided moodily. His vision of space apparently had disturbed him, perhaps seriously. He took little notice of the great thing that was happening, but instead huddled worriedly over his own expanding speculations. Lavon felt the old gap between their minds widening once more.

Now the Bottom was tilting upward again. Lavon had no experience with delta-formation, for no rivulets left his own world, and the phenomenon worried him. But his worries were swept away in wonder as the ship topped the rise and nosed over.

Ahead, the Bottom sloped away again, indefinitely, into glimmering depths. A proper sky was over them once more, and Lavon could see small rafts of plankton floating placidly beneath it. Almost at once, too, he saw several of the smaller kinds of Protos, a few of which were already approaching the ship—

Then the girl came darting out of the depths, her features blurred and distorted with distance and terror. At first she did not seem to see the ship at all. She came twisting and turning lithely through the water, obviously hoping only to throw herself over the mound of the delta and into the savage streamlet beyond.

Lavon was stunned. Not that there were men here—he had hoped for that, had even known somehow that men were everywhere in the universe—but at the girl's single-minded flight toward suicide.

"What—"

Then a dim buzzing began to grow in his ears, and he understood.

"Shar! Than! Stravol!" he bawled. "Break out crossbows and spears! Knock out all the windows!" He lifted a foot and kicked through the port in front of him. Someone thrust a crossbow into his hand.

"What?" Shar blurted. "What's the matter? What's happening?"

"Eaters!"

The cry went through the ship like a galvanic shock. The rotifers back in Lavon's own world were virtually extinct, but everyone knew thoroughly the grim history of the long battle man and Proto had waged against them.

The girl spotted the ship suddenly and paused, obviously stricken with despair at the sight of this new monster. She drifted with her own momentum, her eyes alternately fixed upon the ship and jerking back over her shoulder, toward where the buzzing snarled louder and louder in the dimness.

"Don't stop!" Lavon shouted. "This way, this way! We're friends! We'll help!"

Three great semi-transparent trumpets of smooth flesh bored over the rise, the many thick cilia of their coronas whirring greedily. Dicrans, arrogant in their flexible armor, quarreling thickly among themselves as they moved, with the few blurred, pre-symbolic noises which made up their own language.

Carefully, Lavon wound the crossbow, brought it to his shoulder, and fired. The bolt sang away through the water. It lost momentum rapidly, and was caught by a stray current which brought it closer to the girl than to the Eater at which Lavon had aimed.

He bit his lip, lowered the weapon, wound it up again. It did not pay to underestimate the range; he would have to wait. Another bolt, cutting through the water from a side port, made him issue orders to cease firing "until," he added, "you can see their eyespots."

The irruption of the rotifers decided the girl. The motionless wooden monster was of course strange to her, but it had not yet menaced her—and she must have known what it would be like to have three Dicrans over her, each trying to grab from the others the largest share. She threw herself towards the bull'seye port. The three Eaters screamed with fury and greed and bored in after her.

She probably would not have made it, had not the dull vision of the lead Dicran made out the wooden shape of the ship at the last instant. The Dicran backed off, buzzing, and the other two sheered away to avoid colliding with her. After that they had another argument, though they could hardly have formulated what it was that they were fighting about; they were incapable of exchanging any thought much more complicated than the equivalent of "Yaah," "Drop dead," and "You're another."

While they were still snarling at each other, Lavon pierced the nearest one all the way through with an arablast bolt.

The surviving two were at once involved in a lethal battle over the remains.

"Than, take a party out and spear me those two Eaters while they're still fighting," Lavon ordered. "Don't forget to destroy their eggs, too. I can see that this world needs a little taming."

The girl shot through the port and brought up against the far wall of the cabin, flailing in terror. Lavon tried to approach her, but from somewhere she produced a flake of stonewort chipped to a nasty point. Since she was naked, it was hard to tell where she had been hiding it, but she obviously knew how to use it, and meant to. Lavon retreated and sat down on the stool before his control board, waiting while she took in the cabin, Lavon, Shar, the other pilots, the senescent Para.

At last she said: "Are—you—the gods—from beyond the sky?"

"We're from beyond the sky, all right," Lavon said. "But we're not gods. We're human beings, just like you. Are there many humans here?"

The girl seemed to assess the situation very rapidly, savage though she was. Lavon had the odd and impossible impression that he should recognize her: a tall, deceptively relaxed, tawny woman, not after all quite like this one . . . a woman from another world, to be sure, but still . . .

She tucked the knife back into her bright, matted hair—aha, Lavon thought confusedly, there's a trick I may need to remember—and shook her head.

"We are few. The Eaters are everywhere. Soon they will have the last of us."

Her fatalism was so complete that she actually did not seem to care.

"And you've never cooperated against them? Or asked the Protos to help?"

"The Protos?" She shrugged. "They are as helpless as we are against the Eaters, most of them. We have no weapons that kill at a distance, like yours. And it's too late now for such weapons to do any good. We are too few, the Eaters too many."

Labon shook his head emphatically. "You've had one weapon that counts, all along. Against it, numbers mean nothing. We'll show you how we've used it. You may be able to use it even better than we did, once you've given it a try."

The girl shrugged again. "We dreamed of such a weapon, but never found it. Are you telling the truth? What is the weapon?"

"Brains, of course," Lavon said. "Not just one brain, but a lot of them. Working together. Cooperation."

"Lavon speaks the truth," a weak voice said from the deck.

The Para stirred feebly. The girl watched it with wide eyes. The sound of the Para using human speech seemed to impress her more than the ship itself, or anything else that it contained.

"The Eaters can be conquered," the thin, burring voice said. "The Protos will help, as they helped in the world from which we came. The Protos fought this flight through space, and deprived Man of his records; but Man made the trip without the records. The Protos will never oppose Man again. We have already spoken to the Protos of this world, and have told them that what Man can dream, Man can do. Whether the Protos will it or not.

"Shar—your metal record is with you. It was hidden in the ship. My brothers will lead you to it.

"This organism dies now. It dies in confidence of knowledge, as an intelligent creature dies. Man has taught us this. There is nothing. That knowledge. Cannot do. With it . . . men . . . have crossed . . . have crossed space . . ."

The voice whispered away. The shining slipper did not change, but something about it was gone. Lavon looked at the girl; their eyes met. He felt an unaccountable warmth.

"We have crossed space," Lavon repeated softly.

Shar's voice came to him across a great distance. The young-old man was whispering: "But—have we?"

Lavon was looking at the girl. He had no answer for Shar's question. It did not seem to be important.

BOOK FOUR

WATERSHED

The murmurs of discontent—Capt. Gorbel, being a military man, thought of it as "disaffection"—among the crew of the R.S.S. *Indefeasible* had reached the point where they could no longer be ignored, well before the ship had come within fifty light years of its objective.

Sooner or later, Gorbel thought, sooner or later this idiotic seal-creature is going to notice them.

Capt. Gorbel wasn't sure whether he would be sorry or glad when the Adapted Man caught on. In a way, it would make things easier. But it would be an uncomfortable moment, not only for Hoqqueah and the rest of the pantrope team, but for Gorbel himself. Maybe it would be better to keep sitting on the safety valve until Hoqqueah and the other Altarians were put off on—what was its name again? Oh yes, Earth.

But the crew plainly wasn't going to let Gorbel put it off that long.

As for Hoqqueah, he didn't appear to have a noticing center anywhere in his brain. He was as little discommoded by the emotional undertow as he was by the thin and frigid air the Rigellian crew maintained inside the battlecraft. Secure in his coat of warm blubber, his eyes brown, liquid and merry, he sat in the forward greenhouse for most of each

149

ship's day, watching the growth of the star Sol in the black skies ahead.

And he talked. Gods of all stars, how he talked! Capt. Gorbel already knew more about the ancient—the *very* ancient —history of the seeding program than he had had any desire to know, but there was still more coming. Nor was the seeding program Hoqqueah's sole subject. The Colonization Council delegate had had a vertical education, one which cut in a narrow shaft through many different fields of specialization— in contrast to Gorbel's own training, which had been spread horizontally over the whole subject of spaceflight without more than touching anything else.

Hoqqueah seemed to be making a project of enlarging the Captain's horizons, whether he wanted them enlarged or not.

"Take agriculture," he was saying at the moment. "This planet we're to seed provides an excellent argument for taking the long view of farm policy. There used to be jungles there; it was very fertile. But the people began their lives as farmers with the use of fire, and they killed themselves off in the same way."

"How?" Gorbel said automatically. Had he remained silent, Hoqqueah would have gone on anyhow; and it didn't pay to be impolite to the Colonization Council, even by proxy.

"In their own prehistory, fifteen thousand years before their official zero date, they cleared farmland by burning it off. Then they would plant a crop, harvest it, and let the jungle return. Then they burned the jungle off and went through the cycle again. At the beginning, they wiped out the greatest abundance of game animals Earth was ever to see, just by farming that way. Furthermore the method was totally destructive to the topsoil.

"But did they learn? No. Even after they achieved spaceflight, that method of farming was standard in most of the remaining jungle areas—even though the bare rock was showing through everywhere by that time."

Hoqqueah sighed. "Now, of course, there are no jungles. There are no seas, either. There's nothing but desert, naked rock, bitter cold, and thin, oxygen-poor air—or so the people would view it, if there were any of them left. *Tapa* farming wasn't solely responsible, but it helped."

Gorbel shot a quick glance at the hunched back of Lt. Averdor, his adjutant and navigator. Averdor had managed to avoid saying so much as one word to Hoqqueah or any of the other pantropists from the beginning of the trip. Of course he wasn't required to assume the diplomatic burdens involved—

those were Gorbel's crosses—but the strain of dodging even normal intercourse with the seal-men was beginning to tell on him.

Sooner or later, Averdor was going to explode. He would have nobody to blame for it but himself, but that wouldn't prevent everybody on board from suffering from it.

Including Gorbel, who would lose a first-class navigator and adjutant.

Yet it was certainly beyond Gorbel's authority to order Averdor to speak to an Adapted Man. He could only suggest that Averdor run through a few mechanical courtesies, for the good of the ship. The only response had been one of the stoniest stares Gorbel had ever seen, even from Averdor, with whom the Captain had been shipping for over thirty Galactic years.

And the worst of it was that Gorbel was, as a human being, wholly on Averdor's side.

"After a certain number of years, conditions change on *any* planet," Hoqqueah babbled solemnly, waving a flipper-like arm to include all the points of light outside the greenhouse. He was working back to his primary obsession: the seeding program. "It's only logical to insist that man be able to change with them—or, if he can't do that, he must establish himself somewhere else. Suppose he had colonized only the Earthlike planets? Not even those planets *remain* Earthlike forever, not in the biological sense."

"Why would we have limited ourselves to Earthlike planets in the first place?" Gorbel said. "Not that I know much about the place, but the specs don't make it sound like an optimum world."

"To be sure," Hoqqueah said, though as usual Gorbel didn't know which part of his own comment Hoqqueah was agreeing to. "There's no survival value in pinning one's race forever to one set of specs. It's only sensible to go on evolving with the universe, so as to stay independent of such things as the aging of worlds, or the explosions of their stars. And look at the results! Man exists now in so many forms that there's always a refuge *somewhere* for any threatened people. That's a great achievement—compared to it, what price the old arguments about sovereignty of form?"

"What, indeed?" Gorbel said, but inside his skull his other self was saying: Ah-ha, he smells the hostility after all. Once an Adapted Man, always an Adapted Man—and always fighting for equality with the basic human form. But it's no good, you seal-snouted bureaucrat. You can argue for the rest of your life, but your whiskers will always wiggle when you talk.

And obviously you'll never stop talking.

"And as a military man yourself, you'd be the first to appreciate the military advantages, Captain," Hoqqueah added earnestly. "Using pantropy, man has seized thousands of worlds that would have been inacccessible to him otherwise. It's enormously increased our chances to become masters of the galaxy, to take most of it under occupation *without* stealing anyone else's planet in the process. An occupation without dispossession—let alone without bloodshed. Yet if some race other than man should develop imperial ambitions, and try to annex *our* planets, it will find itself enormously outnumbered."

"That's true," Capt. Gorbel said, interested in spite of himself. "It's probably just as well that we worked fast, way back there in the beginning. Before somebody else thought up the method, I mean. But, how come it *was* us? Seems to me that the first race to invent it should've been a race that already had it—if you follow me."

"Not quite, Captain. If you will give me an example—?"

"Well, we scouted a system once where there was a race that occupied two different planets, not both at the same time, but back and forth," Gorbel said. "They had a life-cycle that had three different forms. In the first form they'd winter over on the outermost of the two worlds. Then they'd change to another form that could cross space, mother-naked, without ships, and spend the rest of the year on the inner planet in the third form. Then they'd change back into the second form and cross back to the colder planet.

"It's a hard thing to describe. But the point is, this wasn't anything they'd worked out; it was natural to them. They'd evolved that way." He looked at Averdor again. "The navigation was tricky around there during the swarming season."

Avedor failed to rise to the bait.

"I see; the point is well taken," Hoqqueah said, nodding with grotesque thoughtfulness. "But let me point out to you, Captain, that being already able to do a thing doesn't aid you in thinking of it as something that needs to be perfected. Oh, I've seen races like the one you describe, too—races with polymorphism, sexual alteration of generation, metamorphosis of the insect life-history type, and so on. There's a planet named Lithia, about forty light years from here, where the dominant race undergoes complete evolutionary recapitulation *after* birth—not before it, as men do. But why should any of them think of form-changing as something extraordinary, and to be striven for? It's one of the commonplaces of their lives, after all."

A small bell chimed in the greenhouse. Hoqqueah got up at once, his movements precise and almost graceful despite his tubbiness. "Thus endeth the day," he said cheerfully. "Thank you for your courtesy, Captain."

He waddled out. He would, of course, be back tomorrow.

And the day after that.

And the next day—unless the crewmen hadn't tarred and feathered the whole bunch by then.

If only, Gorbel thought distractedly, if only the damned Adapts weren't so quick to abuse their privileges! As a delegate of the Colonization Council, Hoqqueah was a person of some importance, and could not be barred from entering the greenhouse except in an emergency. But didn't the man know that he shouldn't use the privilege each and every day, on a ship manned by basic-form human beings most of whom could not enter the greenhouse at all without a direct order?

And the rest of the pantropists were just as bad. As passengers with the technical status of human beings, they could go almost anywhere in the ship that the crew could go—and they did, persistently and unapologetically, as though moving among equals. Legally, that was what they were—but didn't they know by this time that there was such a thing as prejudice? And that among common spacemen the prejudice against their kind—and against any Adapted Man—always hovered near the borderline of bigotry?

There was a slight hum as Averdor's power chair swung around to face the Captain. Like most Rigellian men, the lieutenant's face was lean and harsh, almost like that of an ancient religious fanatic, and the starlight in the greenhouse hid nothing to soften it; but to Capt. Gorbel, to whom it was familiar down to its last line, it looked especially forbidding now.

"Well?" he said.

"I'd think you'd be fed to the teeth with that freak by this time," Averdor said without preamble. "Something's got to be done, Captain, before the crew gets so surly that we have to start handing out brig sentences."

"I don't like know-it-alls any better than you do," Gorbel said grimly. "Especially when they talk nonsense—and half of what this one says about space flight is nonsense, that much I'm sure of. But the man's a delegate of the Council. He's got a right to be up here if he wants to."

"You can bar anybody from the greenhouse in an emergency—even the ship's officers."

"I fail to see any emergency," Gorbel said stiffly.

"This is a hazardous part of the galaxy—potentially, anyhow. It hasn't been visited for millennia. That star up ahead has nine planets besides the one we're supposed to land on, and I don't know how many satellites of planetary size. Suppose somebody on one of them lost his head and took a crack at us as we went by?"

Gorbel frowned. "That's reaching for trouble. Besides, the area's been surveyed recently at least once—otherwise we wouldn't be here."

"A sketch job. It's still sensible to take precautions. If there should be any trouble, there's many a Board of Review that would call it risky to have unreliable, second-class human types in the greenhouse when it breaks out."

"You're talking nonsense."

"Dammit, Captain, read between the lines a minute," Averdor said harshly. "I know as well as you do that there's going to be no trouble that we can't handle. And that no reviewing board would pull a complaint like that on *you* if there were. I'm just trying to give you an excuse to use on the seals."

"I'm listening."

"Good. The *Indefeasible* is the tightest ship in the Rigellian navy, her record's clean, and the crew's morale is almost a legend. We can't afford to start gigging the men for their personal prejudices—which is what it will amount to, if those seals drive them to breaking discipline. Besides, they've got a right to do their work without a lot of seal snouts poking continually over their shoulders."

"I can hear myself explaining that to Hoqqueah."

"You don't need to," Averdor said doggedly. "You can tell him, instead, that you're going to have to declare the ship on emergency status until we land. That means that the pantrope team, as passengers, will have to stick to their quarters. It's simple enough."

It was simple enough, all right. And decidedly tempting.

"I don't like it," Gorbel said. "Besides, Hoqqueah may be a know-it-all, but he's not entirely a fool. He'll see through it easily enough."

Averdor shrugged. "It's your command," he said. "But I don't see what he could do about it even if he did see through it. It'd be all on the log and according to regs. All he could report to the Council would be a suspicion—and they'd probably discount it. Everybody knows that these second-class

154

types are quick to think they're being persecuted. It's my theory that that's why they *are* persecuted, a lot of the time at least."

"I don't follow you."

"The man I shipped under before I came on board the *Indefeasible*," Averdor said, "was one of those people who don't even trust themselves. They expect everybody they meet to slip a knife into them when their backs are turned. And there are always other people who make it almost a point of honor to knife a man like that, just because he seems to be asking for it. He didn't hold that command long."

"I see what you mean," Gorbel said. "Well, I'll think about it."

But by the next ship's day, when Hoqqueah returned to the greenhouse, Gorbel still had not made up his mind. The very fact that his own feelings were on the side of Averdor and the crew made him suspicious of Averdor's "easy" solution. The plan was tempting enough to blind a tempted man to flaws that might otherwise be obvious.

The Adapted Man settled himself comfortably and looked out through the transparent metal. "Ah," he said. "Our target is sensibly bigger now, eh, Captain? Think of it: in just a few days now, we will be—in the historical sense—home again."

And now it was riddles! "What do you mean?" Gorbel said.

"I'm sorry; I thought you knew. Earth is the home planet of the human race, Captain. There is where the basic form evolved."

Gorbel considered this unexpected bit of information cautiously. Even assuming that it was true—and it probably was, that would be the kind of thing Hoqqueah would know about a planet to which he was assigned—it didn't seem to make any special difference in the situation. But Hoqqueah had obviously brought it out for a reason. Well, he'd be trotting out the reason, too, soon enough; nobody would ever accuse the Altarian of being taciturn.

Nevertheless, he considered turning on the screen for a close look at the planet. Up to now he had felt not the slightest interest in it.

"Yes, there's where it all began," Hoqqueah said. "Of course at first it never occurred to those people that they might produce pre-adapted children. They went to all kinds of extremes to adapt their environment instead, or to carry it along with them. But they finally realized that with the planets, that won't work. You can't spend your life in a spacesuit, or under a dome, either.

"Besides, they had had form trouble in their society from their earliest days. For centuries they were absurdly touchy over minute differences in coloring and shape, and even in thinking. They had regime after regime that tried to impose its own concept of the standard citizen on everybody, and enslaved those who didn't fit the specs."

Abruptly, Hoqqueah's chatter began to make Gorbel uncomfortable. It was becoming easier and easier to sympathize with Averdor's determination to ignore the Adapted Man's existence entirely.

"It was only after they'd painfully taught themselves that such differences really don't matter that they could go on to pantropy," Hoqqueah said. "It was the logical conclusion. Of course, a certain continuity of form had to be maintained, and has been maintained to this day. You cannot totally change the form without totally changing the thought processes. If you give a man the form of a cockroach, as one ancient writer foresaw, he will wind up thinking like a cockroach, not like a human being. We recognized that. On worlds where only extreme modifications of the human form would make it suitable—for instance, a planet of the gas giant type —no seeding is attempted. The Council maintains that such worlds are the potential property of other races than the human, races whose psychotypes would not have to undergo radical change in order to survive there."

Dimly, Capt. Gorbel saw where Hoqqueah was leading him, and he did not like what he saw. The seal-man, in his own maddeningly indirect way, was arguing his right to be considered an equal in fact as well as in law. He was arguing it, however, in a universe of discourse totally unfamiliar to Capt. Gorbel, with facts whose validity he alone knew and whose relevance he alone could judge. He was, in short, loading the dice, and the last residues of Gorbel's tolerance were evaporating rapidly.

"Of course there was resistance back there at the beginning," Hoqqueah said. "The kind of mind that had only recently been persuaded that colored men are human beings was quick to take the attitude that an Adapted Man—any Adapted Man—was the social inferior of the 'primary' or basic human type, the type that lived on Earth. But it was also a very old idea on the Earth that basic humanity inheres in the mind, not in the form.

"You see, Captain, all this might still have been prevented, had it been possible to maintain the attitude that changing the form even in part makes a man less of a man than he was in the 'primary' state. But the day has come when that attitude is no longer tenable—a day that is the greatest of all moral watersheds for our race, the day that is to unite all our divergent currents of attitudes toward each other into one common reservoir of brotherhood and purpose. You and I are very fortunate to be on the scene to see it."

"Very interesting," Gorbel said coldly. "But all those things happened a long time ago, and we know very little about this part of the galaxy these days. Under the circumstances—which you'll find clearly written out in the log, together with the appropriate regulations—I'm forced to place the ship on emergency alert beginning tomorrow, and continuing until your team disembarks. I'm afraid that means that henceforth all passengers will be required to stay in quarters."

Hoqqueah turned and arose. His eyes were still warm and liquid, but there was no longer any trace of merriment in them.

"I know very well what it means," he said. "And to some extent I understand the need—though I had been hoping to see the planet of our birth first from space. But I don't think *you* quite understood *me*, Captain. The moral watershed of which I spoke is not in the past. It is now. It began the day that the Earth itself became no longer habitable for the so-called basic human type. The flowing of the streams toward the common reservoir will become bigger and bigger as word spreads through the galaxy that Earth itself has been seeded with Adapted Men. With that news will go a shock of recognition—the shock of realizing that the 'basic' types are now, and have been for a long time, a very small minority, despite their pretensions."

Was Hoqqueah being absurd enough to threaten—an unarmed, comical seal-man shaking a fist at the captain of the *Indefeasible*? Or—

"Before I go, let me ask you this one question, Captain. Down there is your home planet, and my team and I will be going out on its surface before long. Do you dare to follow us out of the ship?"

"And why should I?" Gorbel said.

"Why, to show the superiority of the basic type, Captain," Hoqqueah said softly. "Surely you cannot admit that a pack of seal-men are your betters, on your own ancestral ground!"

He bowed and went to the door. Just before he reached it, he turned and looked speculatively at Gorbel and at Lt.

Averdor, who was staring at him with an expression of rigid fury.

"Or can you?" he said. "It will be interesting to see how you manage to comport yourselves as a minority. I think you lack practice."

He went out. Both Gorbel and Averdor turned jerkily to the screen, and Gorbel turned it on. The image grew, steadied, settled down.

When the next trick came on duty, both men were still staring at the vast and tumbled desert of the Earth.

Other SIGNET Science Fiction You Will Enjoy

☐ **DAVID STARR, SPACE RANGER by Isaac Asimov writing as Paul French.** A clever and brutal scheme by an alien conspiracy to cripple Earth's economic life puts David Starr to work in the first of an exciting series of extra-terrestrial adventures by a master of science fiction.
(#T4849—75¢)

☐ **GALAXIES LIKE GRAINS OF SAND by Brian Aldiss.** An exciting chronicle of eight distant tomorrows—each another step forward into the future reaches of time and space.
(#T4781—75¢)

☐ **THE CONTINENT MAKERS and Other Tales of the Viagens by L. Sprague de Camp.** Collected for the first time in one volume, fantastic adventures from the amazing chronicle of the Age of the Viagens. One of the most remarkable science fiction achievements of all time.
(#Q4825—95¢)

☐ **THE FAR OUT PEOPLE A Science Fiction Anthology edited by Robert Hoskins.** Here is another intriguing volume in this popular series of science fiction anthologies featuring **Isaac Asimov, Chad Oliver and Roger Zelazny.**
(#Q4689—95¢)

THE NEW AMERICAN LIBRARY, INC.,
P.O. Box 999, Bergenfield, New Jersey 07621

Please send me the SIGNET BOOKS I have checked above. I am enclosing $_____(check or money order—no currency or C.O.D.'s). Please include the list price plus 15¢ a copy to cover handling and mailing costs. (Prices and numbers are subject to change without notice.)

Name_____

Address_____

City_____State_____Zip Code_____
Allow at least 3 weeks for delivery